MILE HIGH

B. CRANFORD

This book is a work of fiction. Names, characters, places, and incidents are products of the author's imagination or used fictitiously. Any resemblance to actual events or locales or persons living or dead is entirely coincidental.

Cover Design: Shanoff Designs

Copy Editing: Missy Borucki

Manufactured in the United States

SYNOPSIS

They say time flies when you're having fun, but what about when you're falling in love?

Bianca Evers is recovering from the end of her marriage to her college sweetheart when she's seated next to the sexiest man she's ever seen.

Lucas Hawke is flying home to Australia, still dreaming of something *more* with the right person when he encounters a beautiful woman with sad eyes.

And now they only have fifteen hours to figure out if their connection is worth upgrading—or just a layover in life . . .

For my best friend, Bianca AKA Binky Boodle.
I've loved you for the better part of 20 years and I wouldn't be writing romance if not for you. Thank you for introducing me to Nalini Singh.
And thank you for always being there for me.

1

BIANCA

I COULDN'T STOP TAP, TAP, TAPPING MY PASSPORT AGAINST MY hand. I knew it was a nervous habit, but I couldn't help it.

I *was* nervous, after all. The decision to fly halfway around the world—during the busiest travel time of the year, no less—wasn't one I'd made lightly.

An overhead announcement paged three people late to board their flight, and I took a long, deep breath to try and settle my nerves, my body.

I wasn't afraid to fly—matter of fact I'd just hopped off a flight to LAX from Madison—for as long as I could remember, I'd been traveling via airplane. With family in two different states and living in a third, there was always somewhere to go, someone to see, something to celebrate.

No, I was nervous because this would be my first Christmas without anyone to join in the festivities.

My parents and brothers would be staying in North Carolina, spending the holiday together with my brothers' wives and children. My ex-husband, Mason, was still in South Africa, probably with a new girlfriend by his side.

And I was jumping on a plane and flying to Australia.

Because after a year of heartbreak, spending the biggest holiday of the year away from the places I'd lived with and loved my ex, and all the happy couples that surrounded me, had seemed like a good—if expensive—idea.

"Australia?" My best friend, Ashton, had looked shocked when I'd told her my plans. I knew she'd expected—maybe even hoped—that I would spend Christmas with her and her family, but I didn't want to be the third wheel.

Or, I guess, the seventh wheel, since Ash and her two brothers, Aaron and Austin, all had partners standing by their side.

Just like I used to have.

"Australia," I'd confirmed, offering a cheerful smile and hoping Ash didn't look too deep to see the anger and the pain that lingered below the surface. "I've always wanted to go, you know that. And what could be better for Christmas than spending time in the country that gave us the Hemsworth brothers and Hugh Jackman?"

That comment earned me a laugh, and an eye roll.

"Bianca . . ." Ash trailed off, clearly wanting to ask me about Mason and whether or not I was okay.

"I'm fine, I promise." I'd reached out to place a hand on her arm, needing the contact with the woman who'd been my best friend since the first day of college.

"If you're not, you'll tell me?"

"I wouldn't tell anyone else." The promise had been easy to make, because Ash was my person. The one I confided in. Even when I'd been living in far-flung places, we'd still found a way to stay in contact, to keep up to date with one another.

But this Christmas was to be her first with Andrew—who she'd finally gotten together with fifteen years after they'd first met—and their adorable daughter, Kennedy.

"You'll call me when you're there safely, and every day until you come home." It hadn't been a request, but an order. With her blond curls and sweet smile, Ashton might've looked innocent and kind and chill, but I knew better.

There was a fierce, strong woman under that All-American exterior—the one that had driven her to pursue her motherhood dreams even when she'd been alone, herself at the end of a years-long relationship.

"I promise," I'd repeated, knowing she'd hold me to it. "I'll call and tell you all about the hot Australian Christmas—"

"And the hot Australian men."

Laughing again at the memory of Ashton's need for a daily hot guy update, I continued tap, tap, tapping my passport against my palm. After a mind-numbing three-hour delay, boarding was due to start any minute, and from the looks of the crowded gate seating, it was going to be a full flight.

Very full.

That was fine by me. I didn't mind long flights—this one would be nearly fifteen hours—and I didn't even mind the cramped space.

Nope, all I minded was getting to Australia in one piece, so I could start working on mending my broken heart—and discovering the person I wanted to be now that I was just me.

For so long, I had been a part of a couple, so being alone in the world again was like wearing new shoes. Kind of. I guess you pick new shoes out for yourself, whereas Mason's actions had been the reason for our divorce. But in other ways, the metaphor worked.

You liked what you had on your feet and you wanted to

wear them. But they felt strange, foreign, and maybe even a little painful at first. Until you broke them in and made them yours. *That* is what I wanted to do with my new, Mason-less life.

Make it mine.

"We are now boarding passengers in rows sixty through eighty-five."

The announcement was crackly, but as I'd been listening intently since they first started allowing passengers on board, it was enough to penetrate my thoughts. Normally, I would happily sit and wait until the line had died down—I didn't really understand the mad rush to get to my seat, only to sit there being jostled by people weaving down the aisles, or new passengers needing you to move out of their way—but this time, I was ready.

I needed to escape my thoughts and all the reasons I was running away to Australia. That meant I wanted to be stowing my little red carry-on, hooking my travel pillow around my neck, and settling into my very own version of flight mode as soon as humanly possible.

Like a phone, I would be switched off for the duration, so that when I landed in Melbourne, I would be ready to go. Have a full battery, so to speak.

"Excuse me?" A short, grey-haired man paused next to me, a sheepish smile on his face. "I'm sorry, did you hear what they said? I missed it entirely."

I returned his smile, and gave him the info he was after, waiting until he was on his way to collect his bags before I stood, and wheeled my bag—and myself—over to the line.

"Crowded flight."

This time, it was a woman speaking to me, and her accent was easy to place and a delight to my American ears.

"Sure is. That time of year, I guess." I nodded to her

Australian passport, and asked, "Are you heading home for the holidays, or from vacation?"

"For the holidays. I've lived over here for a while now, but it's always good to get home and see my family." She shrugged. "I just wish it wasn't so bloody expensive."

Laughing, I thought how *not* wrong she was and how lucky I was to be able to afford this last-minute trip. Thank god I had the luxury of running away from my life, if only for a little while.

"You can't just leave, Bianca. We have to talk about this." I heard the echo of Mason's angry words as he'd zipped up his pants and I'd tried to process what my eyes were seeing.

Not wanting that moment—or any of the ones since—to infect my escape, I kept talking to the woman standing ahead of me as we made our way to the front of line. We chatted about nothing much at all, and by the time we were both settled—her a few rows behind me, having wished me a Merry Christmas as I dropped my stuff on my seat—Mason's betrayal was momentarily forgotten, and I was more than ready to get into my flight mode.

But it wasn't to be.

I carefully organized those things I knew I'd need to see me through the lengthy flight—fully-loaded Kindle tucked into the seat pocket, along with my phone and headphones—and stowed my carry-on overhead, then looked at the two empty seats beside me.

Maybe they'll stay empty, I thought wistfully, knowing it was highly unlikely. Perhaps if I wasn't traveling at Christmas—with every other person on the planet.

I people-watched the steady if slow stream of people shuffling past me to their seats, trying to make up their stories. It was a game I'd played before when I was bored—one Ashton and I had actually played together during long road trips with the passengers of passing cars—and it was fun.

Especially since I always gave my targets a happy ending. (Not that kind, get your mind out of the gutter.)

Two women laughed together, leaning in close, before taking their seats in the row in front of me. I decided this was their first Christmas together and they were just starting a round-the-world trip.

A family—mother, father, and two kids already in pajamas—walked by and sat a couple of rows behind me and in the center of the plane. In my head, the kids carefully wrote to Santa asking him to remember they were going to be visiting their grandparents in Australia for the first time. Of course, he'd know that and bring them extra-special presents, because why not?

What about me? I wondered. What did the people passing by see in me?

"Maybe if you smiled at me like you were happy to see me, like you cared whether I came home, then I wouldn't have looked somewhere else for affection."

Mason's words—a cut that felt deep and still stingingly new, even though it had been months since I'd last seen or spoken to him.

Shaking off the mental intrusion of my ex, I watched a few more people move around our area of the plane, and was just judging the looks and formulating the story of the man who was settling into the aisle seat of my row—*newly married businessman returning home early to surprise his wife for Christmas, perhaps?*—when the second of my seatmates arrived.

The one who'd be in the middle seat and therefore sitting next to me for the next fifteen hours.

And damn if he wasn't the sexiest man I'd ever seen.

I WAS STARING.

I knew I was and still couldn't seem to stop myself.

Focus, Bianca, I scolded myself. Although, actually, I should have been telling myself not to focus. Or focus on something other than his ridiculously good looks. I wanted to bite my lip when he licked his own—they were light pink and full and kissable and *why was I thinking about his lips?!*

And then . . . ugh, and then he reached overhead to stow his battered looking backpack, and I caught a glimpse of muscled abs. And a teasing line of hair disappearing below the waistline of his sweatpants.

Grey sweatpants.

I have no idea why I thought that was hot as hell, but I did, and I wasn't about to lie to myself about it. They sat low and—

He was looking at me.

Oh shit, and I was clearly looking at him. Not just at him, either. I was basically staring at his dick like it held the answers to all life's questions as I admired the fit of those cotton pants.

They fit perfectly, in case you were wondering.

Releasing my lower lip, because yes, at some point I'd acted on that impulse to bite it while I admired him—as if being caught staring wasn't awkward enough—I quickly looked away. And tried to decide if I should just brazen it out and say hello or spend the next fifteen hours pretending he wasn't seated right next to me.

Because he was. Of course, he was. I was at the window, he was in the middle, and the third person in our row would act like the guard keeping us in place. I was going to be brushing arms with this man for the duration.

Why does this flight have to be so long? I laughed quietly to myself, knowing that I normally wouldn't care—not about the flight time and not about being caught staring. Well, maybe about the lip biting, but the staring in general was fine.

Just. Like. That. Man. If ever a man was made to be looked at and objectified, it was the one I was getting ready to relinquish an arm rest to. But the disappointment of the last couple of years, coupled with the words Mason had flung at me when defending himself, had changed me enough to know that I was uncomfortable because I didn't know how to act around hot, presumably single men.

Scrap that. I didn't know how to act around hot men, single or not. Because it wasn't about whether anything was going to or could happen, it was about the fact that I'd been in a relationship for the better part of fifteen years—thirteen of them married—and now I wasn't.

The hot men might not be any different, but *I* was.

I'd been practically a kid when I'd met Mason and fallen in love. It had taken months for that love to grow from the friendship we'd formed on the first day of our sophomore year of college, but when we'd both realized our relationship had changed, it seemed like it had always been meant to be.

"You're the one, Bianca. I didn't realize it at first, but now I know, I can't stop thinking about it. Our future. Our forever."

I sighed at the bittersweet memory that time had turned more bitter than sweet. This trip was supposed to be about getting away from my broken marriage and my broken heart and trying something new. Something for just me.

And yet, here I was, thinking about him. Thinking about the day he'd proposed to me and promised me a lifetime.

All because I couldn't handle the handsome-as-fuck

man currently ripping open the plastic-wrapped blanket beside me.

As subtly as I could, I looked him over again, determined to find something about him that wasn't visually perfect. Something that made me a little more comfortable about sitting next to him as we crossed the International Date Line.

The International Date-Me Line.

Because, failing that, I could only hope that he was a dickhead or an asshole or maybe even a total tool.

He'd sunk his teeth into his bottom lip in an adorable look of concentration, having draped the blanket over his legs and grabbed the emergency exit card from the seat pocket in front of him. I'd never seen anyone give that safety card so much attention and something about that was endearing.

A little weird, if I was honest, but endearing.

For the record, I knew I shouldn't judge, because for all I knew it was his first time flying and he was nervous, but . . . I couldn't help it. I was judging him, and he was getting a ten-point-zero in the *damn, that's cute* event.

I looked away from the mouth that I would wager good money could move from sweet to sexy in a heartbeat and looked over his stubbled jaw. It was square and masculine and something about it made me want to trail my fingers along it to trace its shape.

Girl, you need to settle down. Not only was I visually molesting this man, I was thinking like a fifteen-year-old with their first real crush. I needed to give him an imaginary happily-ever-after that included a wife who was the kind of gorgeous that only a man like him could even look at, five kids including two sets of twins, and a house full of rescue animals.

Because that would *definitely* ensure I stopped staring. For sure.

Except . . . his hair was dark and although I couldn't see exactly what shade it was in the terrible airplane lighting, I could tell that it looked soft and inviting. The kind of hair that a woman could grab onto while his face was buried between her thighs, his tongue working overtime to give her an orgasm or two.

I scolded myself, sighing inwardly—because I didn't want him to hear me, obviously—and turning back toward the window. I'd found nothing that made him less than perfect, which meant I was now officially team let-this-hot-dude-be-a-jackass.

"G'day."

I snapped my head around to look at him, the deep perfection (of course it was perfection, *of course it was*) of his voice coupled with the obviously Australian greeting and the hint of that distinctive accent making my thighs clench. My heart racing from the acknowledgement, I smiled at him, nodding in a polite greeting. It wasn't that I didn't want to say "G'day" back, it was more that I couldn't. My voice had left the building—okay, the plane—along with my ability to act like an adult rather than a schoolgirl with a crush.

I opened my mouth in an attempt to say something, all the while praying that it didn't come out stuttered and/or squeaky, but he beat me to it.

"I'm Lucas. Australian," he added, pointing at himself. It was such an odd way of introducing himself that my smile grew wider, my awkwardness unlocking enough that I could reply.

"Bianca. American." Not a squeak or a stutter to be found, which made me mentally fist pump.

Lucas held out his hand for a shake and I'm almost ashamed to admit I reached for it like it was a lifeline. A little zing of awareness rippled through me when our palms met, and I wondered if he felt it too, or if I was making too much of this simple, friendly greeting.

Naturally, my brain chose that moment to remind me that I had never felt this kind of zing with Mason. Certainly not the first time we met or touched. Not that we were completely zing-free, but there was something about this one that was . . . I don't know. *Zingier*.

"Well, Bianca. Looks like we have about fifteen hours to get to know one another"—he tilted his head just a little and I mimicked the move, inviting him to keep talking, our hands still joined between us—"so I sure hope you liked what you saw when you were checking me out just now."

2

BIANCA

I WAS HEARING THINGS. I HAD TO BE.

There was no way he'd just blatantly, brazenly called out my ogling. Sure, my ogling had probably—okay, certainly—been as blatant and as brazen as his question, but still . . .

Drawing my hand back from Lucas', I narrowed my eyes and gave him a chance to change what he'd just said. "I'm sorry?"

"Don't be sorry. When a girl as pretty as you looks at me"—he shrugged easily, like he wasn't completely calling me out for objectifying him—"it feels good."

I wasn't prepared for such an honest and, frankly, amusing answer. Probably the fact that he'd said it in that yummy accent—"pretty" sounded like "priddy" and it made goosebumps rise along my arms—helped to make the impertinent question amiable instead of arrogant.

Okay, it was still arrogant, but charmingly so.

I was about two-point-five seconds away from asking him if he really thought I was pretty, which I know, I know, I shouldn't have focused on, when we were interrupted by the flight attendant. She was doing her last-minute checks, leaning a little way over the man in our aisle seat to address Lucas. "Sir, you need to make sure your seat is upright," she said, smiling at him before waiting for him to adjust his seat.

Naturally, because I knew nothing about the man, had actually only said four words to him, and because two could play that game—he'd quite clearly been teasing me just now—I decided to take the opportunity to rib him. "Ooh, you're in trouble already. Are you sure you're going to make it through the entire flight without getting thrown in the lock-up?"

I thought he might laugh. Had, in fact, hoped for it. Surely a man who introduces himself and then immediately follows it up with a brash question could take a joke, right?

Apparently, *wrong*. Because instead of laughing along with me or calling me out for a fairly lame attempt at teasing, Lucas turned to me with a straight face and a grim look in his eyes.

Green. In case you were keeping track, his eyes were green. Just another thing that made him stupidly attractive.

"Excuse me?" He was giving *me* another chance this time —and I wasn't exactly sure what I'd said to upset him, so I carefully repeated what I'd said, hoping that it would be funnier to him the second time around.

"Are you sure you're going to make it through the entire flight without getting thrown in the lock-up? Tell me, are you a lifelong criminal or . . . ?"

It wasn't. Funnier, that is. It was more awkward though, especially since I added onto my original comment, so that was fun. Not.

"Just because we started as a colony of convicts, doesn't mean we're all criminals. Jesus." His eyes rolled in exasperation. "Americans sure do love to stereotype, don't they?"

I could feel the mortification start to build in me. I'd

insulted him. I'd *insulted* him?! I couldn't believe it. I certainly hadn't intended it. How could I have? Like, if I was going to stereotype an Australian, I'd have imagined him wrangling crocodiles and yelling "Crikey" every other minute.

"I'm so sorry. Oh, shit. I didn't—that wasn't what I–I'm sorry." My smile was big—too big—mostly because I was waiting for him to, I don't know, call the flight attendant back and demand to swap seats, but instead, he simply held my gaze.

I wanted to cry. Maybe stomp my foot a little, because being misunderstood sucked. And being misunderstood while just a little bit (read: a *lot*) stressed majorly sucked. It wasn't like I was inexperienced with stereotyping and assumptions and bad behavior. The fifteen-hour flight probably wasn't enough time to run through all the shit I'd dealt with over the years from people who were determined to only see what they wanted to see—if they saw anything at all.

Except . . . I'd never really been on the other side of it before. Not like this. I could own having stereotyped people before, because who hasn't? But being called out for behaving badly and making base assumptions? No, definitely not.

Lucas' green eyes, so incredibly intense, suddenly morphed into eyes of laughter. His mouth, which had been a grim, set line, curved into a smile that showcased some really perfect teeth.

Australians might have criminals for ancestors and a bad habit of fooling with dangerous animals, but they didn't have the stereotypical teeth problems their British counterparts had.

Shit, shit. I was doing it again—in my head, at least, but still . . .

"Hey, wait." My eyes narrowed, much like Lucas' had done only moments earlier, and I stared at him again, taking in the laugh lines that had formed around those lips, the mischievous glint in his eyes. "You were messing with me?"

He pursed those lips, possibly to hold back a laugh, and nodded. "I'm sorry, I couldn't help myself." He at least had the good sense to look abashed when I reached out and backhanded his bicep. Not too hard, but hard enough to tell him I was *not* amused.

Except I was, a little.

He'd got me good, after all, and the quick, easy way he'd let me in on his secret told me that he was just being playful, just joking around. If it'd been anyone else, maybe I wouldn't have been so forgiving, but there was just something so irresistible about the way he started laughing when my hand made contact with the firm muscle of his upper arm.

And yes, I absolutely did notice the strength in that arm.

It was one more perfect thing about him.

Damn it.

"You're an asshole." I stated it boldly, something that the pre-divorce Bianca might have done, but not this new, cheated-on Bianca. She was the one who shrunk back and wanted to cry—the one who took things a little too hard and sometimes a little too seriously. So, yeah, calling Lucas an asshole so brazenly felt good. Score one for this trip helping me find myself again; we hadn't even taken off yet, though we had begun to taxi, and I was already calling out a relative stranger.

He deserved it though, no matter how charmingly arrogant and goddamn perfect he was.

"Yeah," he replied, looking chagrined, "I am. But it's better that you know that about me now, before you get too attached."

I thought about giving him a second backhanded slap to the arm—not just to cop a feel of that muscle, but because he deserved it, the jerk. In the end, though, I decided against it.

Unsubtle leering followed by muscle groping disguised as assault was probably not the greatest way for this budding whatever-it-was to take-off. That didn't mean I was just going to let it go, though. "I can't believe you did that to me." I crossed my arms in defense and glared at him, waiting for an explanation.

"I'm sorry," he said again, remorse evident in his tone, even though those green eyes still held a hint of amusement. "Teasing is kind of my thing. Just ask my sister."

"I was seriously horrified that I'd upset you!" I couldn't help the way my voice pitched higher at the end of my sentence, and of course, the sexy asshole beside me just smirked. "It's not funny. Jerk," I added, my declaration belied by the humor in my voice.

"Not even a little bit funny? Like, a little bit?" He held two fingers an inch apart, squinting one eye and scrunching up his nose. "Come on, a little bit," he repeated.

I shook my head despite the fact I was mere seconds away from breaking into laughter myself. Honestly, I couldn't remember the last time I'd laughed with someone other than Ashton and her family. The Andrews family—which included partners and children and friends—could turn any situation from fraught to fucking hilarious in moments, given half the chance.

They'd love Lucas.

The thought was unbidden and unexpected and (mostly) unwanted.

There was no reason for me to be imagining Lucas sitting in the center of that group of people, his Australian accent bouncing off the walls of Ashton's bar, The Avenue, as he told them about the time he'd fooled me on an airplane.

"No shit, she just looked at me, horror dawning on her face that she'd totally put her foot in her mouth, and it was all I could do not to break character immediately," he'd say, to a chorus of laughter and ribbing.

Except I was imagining it, and it was that visual—of this beautiful, teasing man joking with my friends—that set me off.

It started with a giggle, which soon became out-of-control laughter.

Making mental apologies to the couple seated in front of me and the family behind and over, I sent a small prayer up that the other passengers weren't trying to rest already. Because they definitely wouldn't be able to with the noise we were making.

That *I* was making.

Stuttering, I repeated, "It-it's not funny," in the hopes that saying it twice would send the message to my own brain to shut up. It didn't work.

"If it's not funny," Lucas countered, "then why are you laughing?"

It took me way, *way* longer than I'd like to admit to answer his question, because my laughter had become that kind of hysterical that bubbled over again the minute you thought you'd gotten it under control.

"You're still laughing," he pointed out, a chuckle in his voice, which only set me off again.

"It was definitely funny, huh?" He used his knee to nudge mine a little, another zing of awareness shooting through me and halting my hysteria for a hot minute.

Not long enough though, because within a couple of heartbeats, I started to lose it again. And when I finally *did* manage to stumble out a response, it wasn't in answer to that question. "Yes."

"Yes?" He frowned, his body having remained angled toward mine the entire time we laughed, our knees still in contact from that nudge. You know, the zingy one. The one that made me feel more wanted than anything Mason had done for me in years.

Maybe ever.

I smiled, taking a long, deep breath and forcing myself to finish calming down enough to repeat my answer in a more composed voice.

"Yes," I said. We were already nearly fifteen minutes into the flight, the plane having begun to level off, but I'd finally remembered the question he'd asked me as he'd held my hand and decided to give it to him straight. "Yes, Lucas. I liked what I saw very, very much."

3

LUCAS

I COULDN'T BELIEVE MY LUCK. PLANE THIS BIG, AND I WAS sitting next to the woman I'd been unable to keep my eyes off of in the terminal.

Bianca.

She was beautiful. Easily the most beautiful woman I'd ever seen, which was why I'd been watching her while we sat at the gate, waiting for our flight.

At first glance, I'd assumed she was with the man seated beside her in the terminal and I'd experienced a pang of regret. Which was stupid, really. All I knew about her was that she was a stunner—skin like milk chocolate, lips that begged to be kissed, and her hair . . .

Bloody hell, that hair was the stuff of fantasies. Thick and curly, it surrounded her head like a . . . I don't know . . . like a halo or something.

And the guy beside her—he'd leaned close with a smile that said he knew something I didn't, and I'd reached the inevitable conclusion that she was with him.

Not *his*, though. She didn't look like a woman who could ever really be owned.

I'd sat there like a stalker or a peeping Tom, watching her as she occasionally interacted with him, until finally he'd said something, made her smile, and walked away, his backpack slung over his shoulder.

After that, I didn't know what to make of her, except that she was clearly nervous, her passport tapping repeatedly against her palm. I'd wanted to go soothe her, get a closer look, but instead I'd forced myself to make one last stop at the toilets before boarding completed. By the time I'd made it back to the gate, she'd disappeared among the crowd of people queued up to board.

I wouldn't see her again, I'd assumed. A miracle, I'd told myself, is what it would take to locate her among the dozens of people still waiting to board—not to mention the ones already on the plane.

As soon as I'd arrived at my seat, I'd realized I'd gotten my miracle. There she was, sitting at the window, in the row that matched my boarding pass.

If I'd offered a silent and slightly crude note of thanks to some random higher power, who'd ever know?

I was set to wow her with my winning personality—read: the looks I'd been told more than once could get me any girl I wanted—until I'd finally, *finally,* gotten a good look at her up close. And I realized something that made my fists clench involuntarily.

This gorgeous woman who'd jolted my system the second I'd laid eyes on her, she had the saddest eyes I'd ever seen.

What made you sad, pretty girl?

Her eyes weren't so sad at the moment though, which meant my joke had worked. It'd been a gamble, teasing her into thinking she'd offended me. Especially after I'd called her out on giving me the onceover, which was actually more of a three-times-over. But what the hell was I supposed to do? She'd turned her gaze to me immediately, and it'd felt like something snapped into place.

Just think about that for a sec, and tell me if you'd have been able to play off being lip-bitingly lusted over—because, hell yes, she'd bit that lush bottom lip—by the woman you'd been mentally falling into lust with for a solid hour or two already. But she hadn't punched me when I'd made it known I'd noticed her attention. And my subsequent teasing had paid off in a big way when she'd laughed so hard, she couldn't stop.

Of course, she'd got her own back when her eyes—which were the rich brown of dark chocolate and held what I'd somehow recognized as pain—had danced as she told me she'd liked what she'd seen when she'd checked me out.

All that was just step one in my hastily formed plan to make her smile, and make it reach those sad, sweet eyes. Which meant that now I had to come up with step two.

Heads up, step two might just have to be "give it a red hot go."

A master tactician, I was not.

"So, Bianca," I said, after failing to come up with a decent reply to her confession she'd found me all right—more than all right—to look at. "What's taking you to my home country?"

Even her shrug was pretty, and the fact I thought that was the first—okay, more like fourth or fifth—clue that I was maybe, kinda, sorta fucked when it came to this woman.

"It's a long story."

"We have hours. A long story is probably a good way to kill some time."

She turned her head away for a second, and when she

brought her eyes back around to face me, some of that sadness had reappeared.

It made me unreasonably, irrationally angry. Something made her hurt and I found I really didn't like it. This woman—she ignited all my possessive protective urges.

"I just needed a break, I guess. It's-it hasn't been the best year."

"I'm assuming that's your version of 'Once upon a time,' and the long story you started is just beginning?" I waited to see her reaction to that—a smile, *yes*—then added, "Wait, should I call the flight attendant back? See if she can scrounge up some popcorn?"

She giggled, and yeah, it was definitely a giggle. A cute little sound, not like the laughter that had turned hysterical and—I dunno if she'd realized this or not—drawn stares from a few of the people seated nearby.

The man who was seated next to me had been looking, no doubt. I'd turned when I'd heard his low "Jesus," to see if he was going to be a total prick and say something to her. But yeah, nah—he was looking at her, as smitten as I seemed to be.

She touched her hand to my forearm with a warmth that gave me no choice but to bring my attention back to her, to that giggle. "I don't think this is a popcorn story, Lucas."

"Well, shit. A beer? Some wine? A jack and coke?" I listed a few more boozy options and her smile grew.

Her eyes were still sad though. Still, "give it a red hot go" wasn't a step to be rushed.

"I think I'll pass on the alcohol, but thanks for offering."

"No worries. You change your mind, just lemme know. I'm an expert at button pressing." I pointed at the call light on the remote that was embedded in the seat arm.

"I can see that about you," she replied quickly, and I knew she'd caught my double meaning.

I'm going to press as many of your buttons as I can for the next few hours.

Of course, I didn't say that, because that would've been stupid, but I couldn't stop myself thinking it. Or stop myself from inevitably focusing on one button in particular I wanted to press. And if it's not readily apparent which "button" that might be . . . well, anyway. I knew I shouldn't have been thinking about her like that, I just didn't know how to stop myself. Deciding to go with the age-old trick of deflection, I tried to get our conversation—read: myself—back on track. "So, back to this long story. Way I figure it, we have about fourteen hours."

"Actually, it's more like thirteen."

"What?"

"They have flight time in the corner of the screen, see?" She leaned over me a little to point to the little timer on the top right side of the small screen in the seat back in front of me.

"Huh, I've never noticed that before."

"Sorry," she grimaced, and yep, shockingly, she was still fucking beautiful. "Now you'll never stop noticing. I think I just made this your longest flight ever."

"Huh?" Realizing I sounded a little dense, I smiled, trying to force my brain to work past the fact she was the hottest woman I'd ever seen and follow her thought process instead.

Thankfully, she took mercy on me and explained. "You'll keep looking at it, and time will slow to a crawl."

"Oh, right." Yeah, that totally made sense and I felt like a bit of a dick for not making that connection. "That's okay, I can handle a slow-moving clock."

I had the feeling that time would probably go pretty bloody quickly when I was talking to her, and since I didn't want that, the idea of time slowing to a crawl was welcome.

"I still feel bad."

I looked over at her. "You'll just have to distract me from the clock, I guess."

"Uh oh, big responsibility."

"You have no idea. I have the attention span of a gnat." I paused. "Assuming gnats have low attention spans. It sounds like the kind of bug that would flit from one place to the next, totally forgetting everything that just happened, but I am not a—whatever someone is called that knows all about gnats."

"An entomologist?"

"I'm not wowing you with my brains right now, am I?" I wanted to tell her I was smarter than this. That normally, with anyone else in the world, I'd have had no trouble following their thought process. I'd probably also mention that I *did* actually know that entomology was the study of insects, even if I only knew that because of Gil Grissom from the original *CSI*.

Except she smiled at me, and my train of thought went haywire again.

I sucked in a breath at how pretty, how *stunning* her smile was, and took a deep breath to try to regulate my thoughts. Not that it helped—her scent was, like the rest of her, intoxicating.

She smelled so good—not that dry, stale aeroplane smell; more like a garden or something—and it took me a moment to recognize what I was smelling. When I did, though, it made my heart do something funny in my chest.

Lavender.

It reminded me of my childhood and of my mum

putting drops of oil into her diffuser with the small tea light candle.

It made *me* smile this time. A happy memory, like so many others from when I was a kid. "You smell good," I told Bianca, because I couldn't not tell her.

Not when it might make those eyes a little happier.

"Like lavender," I added, because why not double down on it? I'd already told her I'd been smelling her like a weirdo after making it clear I was not the sharpest tool in the shed.

Except I don't think she thought I was weird, because she gave me another wide, bright smile—one that reached her eyes—and said, "It *is* lavender! I have a hand cream I use, and it smells so good. It's also great for relaxation and sleeping, which is why I brought it with me. I thought it'd help me rest on the flight."

"But you can't rest—at least, not until you've told me this long story you promised me." I raised an eyebrow at her, and she gave me an epic eye roll. Seriously, I don't think anyone should underestimate it. I lost sight of those sad eyes for a beat because I'm convinced she rolled them all the way to the back of her head.

"Hey, don't you roll your eyes at me, young lady." I said it in a voice that was supposed to mimic Mum telling my little sister off and designed to get another giggle from Bianca.

It worked. Of course, it fucking did.

Not even two hours in—and at least half of that time was spent on inconsequential small talk and getting settled in—and I was already reading this woman right. My very mature response to that was a fist pump. An internal one because there was really no need to let her see *exactly* how much of an idiot I was. Not completely. Not right away.

I'd save it for hour ten, when she was too delirious from all the flying to let it bother her.

"Sorry," she replied in a tone that was not sorry at all and played into my "Mum voice."

Cute.

"You should be. Now, stop trying to distract me. I wanna hear this long story, and I wanna hear it now."

Her eyes fell closed, as she breathed in deeply. She was clearly steeling herself to share this story with me, and I wondered if maybe I shouldn't have pushed her. Except when she opened those sad eyes, they looked like they were on fire, and when she opened her mouth, I knew her "long story" was going to be very interesting.

"Well, it all started when my husband decided to stick his dick into the lovely twenty-two-year-old daughter of his boss."

4

BIANCA

I FELT LUCAS TENSE BESIDE ME AS I BRAZENLY ANNOUNCED that Mason had betrayed me. I glanced around, quickly checking to see if we were disturbing the other passengers, relieved to see that most were still awake. Likely waiting for the flight attendants to start circulating dinner, which was due to happen at any moment.

Making a point to keep my voice low, I started at the beginning. "Mason and I met in college, and had been married for"—I paused, unable to hold in the sigh that always came with the memory of how many years I'd wasted on my ex—"thirteen years when I found out."

"I don't understand, Ash. I thought, I thought we'd made it. I thought we were safe because . . . because . . ."

I closed my eyes as the memory of trying to make sense of Mason's betrayal—sounding off about it to the person I trusted most to give it to me straight—halted my story though it had barely begun.

"*Wanker,*" Lucas muttered beside me, a frown marring his face. His deep, accented voice reminded me of the way Ashton had called Mason a "complete and utter asshole."

Not because they sounded the same, but because Lucas looked angry on my behalf, just like my best friend had. Almost as if the idea of anyone hurting me or taking advantage of me was so counter to his own instincts, that he wanted to rage. It was . . . gratifying.

"Pretty much, yeah," I agreed, forcing myself to push away the memories that wanted to impede on story time. "He—Mason—is an engineer, and his job took us all over the world. He could've traveled without me, but since I'm a graphic designer, my work comes with a certain amount of flexibility. I can work anywhere there's a power outlet and halfway decent internet connection."

"Like Australia?"

"Assuming you have the internet down under," I joked, smiling at him.

The smile he gave me right back was like a punch to the stomach. Wide and amused and striking. "We do, but it might struggle to meet your 'halfway decent' requirement."

"Really?" I asked, surprised. Mason and I had been in South Africa when I'd discovered him and Lindsey, and the internet connection had been pretty damn good.

Too bad the rest of my time there was less so.

"Yeah, it's a fuckin' joke." He shook his head like he couldn't believe it himself, then said, "But whatever, keep going."

"Right." I steeled myself with a steadying breath and by pulling my shoulders back. This trip was about me, and I wasn't going to let my posture slump because of some bad times. "So. We traveled a lot. And we always made a point of spending time together, even when his work hours were long and exhausting. I won't go into too many details, but as a wastewater process engineer, he worked on and with equipment for safely treating it." I rocked my hand in an "or thereabouts" gesture. "We were in South Africa and had been for, god, a year?"

"Did you like it there?"

"I missed home, but it wasn't bad. It was just . . . a long way from my family and friends, which is why I really noticed when he wasn't around as much."

Hardly at all, as a matter of fact.

"He was with the twenty-two-year-old?"

"Not at first, although I can see why you'd think that. I honestly believe that when he said he was busy, he was genuinely busy." I didn't add that I had to believe that for my own sanity, because if I traveled down that path, I'd start questioning everything about my marriage. And questioning just the last few years was hard enough. "His company was overseeing upgrades to an older treatment plant and he was needed a lot. I knew before we left the States that it wouldn't be like some of his other, cushier placements."

"I can't help it that my job needed my attention."

"More than me?"

"You acted like you didn't want it or me when I was here."

Lucas touched a tentative hand to mine. "Bianca? Are you okay?"

"Sorry, I just . . . he said he was busy, and that his job needed his attention. But then, after, I think that was just a convenient excuse."

I turned my head away from Lucas' intense green stare, relieved when he pulled his hand back. Picturing myself sitting in the small apartment Mason and I had shared—trying to read a book, wondering when he'd be home—I thought again about his accusations that I didn't give him my time when his was free.

"He said it was my fault," I murmured, watching in fascination as Lucas rolled his shoulders and sucked in a hard breath, as if he was offended. Waving my hand to cast off those last words, I tried to play like it was no big deal. "I didn't give him the attention he wanted when he was home. Sometimes because of the things I'd taken on to occupy my time. Sometimes, he was only home when I was asleep." I attempted a laugh. "And snoring, probably."

"Snoring isn't a reason to cheat, Bianca. Neither is you finding ways to fill the gap he left when he wasn't home."

They were true words said in a harsh tone, and something about hearing Lucas' conviction made me share a little more. "He said I didn't smile at him like I used to. That I didn't seem to care that he was home less and less, because I never said anything. But he never said anything either?" I heard the hitch in my voice, yet to my horror, I kept talking. In for a penny, I guess. "I thought I was being supportive, that if I could survive not seeing him and not give him a reason to think I was struggling, I was doing him a favor. Giving him one less thing to worry about."

So naïve. I'd been so fucking naïve.

"Hey." Lucas' voice was low and close, and the wisp of his warm breath across my cheek told me he'd moved in closer. "I get it now. You don't have to tell me the rest."

I turned back toward him, our faces only inches apart. He was even more handsome up close, concern and anger warring for dominance on his face. Reaching inside myself, I pushed back against the emotions trying to shake my foundation. "I guess the story isn't as long as I thought. The rest is pretty simple. His boss came out to visit and brought his daughter—who was working as his assistant for the trip—with him. She was supposed to be learning the business from the bottom up, I think."

I squinted, trying to remember even though the details

weren't actually all that important. "They met. She had lots of time and questions for him, he apparently lied to her about me, and a few weeks later, I walked in on them in his office."

"I'm guessing they weren't discussing water processing," Lucas interjected dryly.

I laughed without humor. "Well, he *did* say she was 'so wet' for him"—I shuddered at the memory—"but that was about the extent of it."

"What a cunt." Lucas' lip was curled in distaste, but his eyes, when they met mine, were caring. Like he knew the memory was unpleasant, to say the least.

I nodded, a corner of my mind reminding me that Australians had the tendency to use the c-word a lot more liberally than most. He wasn't wrong. "He told me I had to let him explain, I told him not to come home, and a couple of days later, *she* came to see me. I was already packing my shit up and planning to head home."

"Lick your wounds?"

"It was either that or exact revenge on him," I replied, aiming for nonchalance and taking a little pride in the fact that I took the high road. "Not that I wasn't tempted by the idea of revenge, because I was."

"Don't tell me you came up with a revenge plan and didn't see it through." Lucas clutched a hand to his chest. "What a waste."

His teasing tone despite the fact our conversation had turned heavy made me confess something I hadn't even told Ashton. "Did you ever read the story about the jilted spouse who left rotting seafood in the curtain rods?"

"No, I don't think so."

"It's exactly what it sounds like—her ex got the house, so she ate caviar or something, shoved the leftovers in the hollow curtain rods, packed up her life and left. Eventually, they sold the place back to her because of the stench, which she was able to get rid of like that." I snapped my fingers.

Lucas made a face that illustrated exactly what he thought of the story—amusement and disgust, which summed up my feelings about it too. "I take it you didn't follow through."

"Well, no. I thought about it a lot. But it wasn't our place and it wouldn't have been fair to the owners."

"That was nice of you."

"I'm a nice person."

"I believe it."

Our eyes locked as pleasure suffused my body at the fact he seemed to have no doubt I was a good human. Forcing my gaze away before the moment could become too fraught, I decided to elaborate on my surprise visitor. "Lindsey—that was her name. She came to apologize, to explain that she'd believed him when he'd said we were separating, otherwise she wouldn't have pursued him."

Lucas took the change in subject back to my story in stride. "Did you believe her?"

"Yes. The thing is, even if she was the aggressor, ultimately, *he* was the one who cheated on me. Who broke his promise. And she-she seemed so sad. It was impossible to ignore it. I think . . . I think she really cared about him."

"Most women wouldn't be so forgiving. Or believing, actually."

"Maybe not. But I'd met her once or twice in the past at company events, and she was always friendly. She never struck me as malicious?" It came out as a question, because I couldn't think of how to explain it, except for the fact I knew.

I *knew.* Mason was the one at fault and she, Lindsey, was

just another person who'd been hurt by his selfishness. Another woman who'd been naïve.

I didn't like to think of Lindsey too much, because even though I knew she'd been hurt too, I still thought of the pain as mostly mine. After all, she'd lost what amounted to a fledging relationship, while I'd lost more than a decade of history and my ability to trust not only Mason, but myself.

I was working on believing in myself again, and this trip was part of it. But I couldn't even think of trusting another man. Not after Mason had given me all the poetic words in the beginning and stripped away my pride in the end.

"Trust me with your heart, Bianca. I promise I'll take care of it."

"So, then what?" Lucas asked, his interruption to my thoughts welcome. "You flew home?"

"Not right away, no. I came home not long before my best friend had her first child, though. I wasn't sure if I wanted to face my family and my failure—"

"*His* failure," Lucas corrected me.

"—but I couldn't miss Ash having her baby." Turning and reaching for the seat pocket in front of me, I grabbed my phone. "You have to see my niece, Kennedy. She's perfect."

Lucas stopped me with a hand to my arm, and I felt the warmth of his touch spread through my body. It was comforting, and familiar, and I was tempted to shrug it off for exactly those reasons.

I didn't need to be noticing the way his touch made me feel. I'd just told this man my sad story of marital demise, a story that still had the power to shake me to my core. It should've been a reminder that I didn't know him. Besides, hadn't I just been thinking about how I couldn't trust anymore? There was no reason to give this man the benefit of the doubt.

Except for the fact it felt like it was out of my control.

"Bianca?" His voice was whisper-quiet, no doubt in respect to the people around us who were settling in for the long flight, or just starting the meal that the flight attendants were now handing out. "I know that you know he's a dick-head, but did you also know that you're better off without him?"

I didn't turn back toward him, making a noncommittal sound instead. I suddenly felt weary. And with that weariness came the doubt that told me I'd never get those wasted years back—and that I'd never find another person to love.

"Bianca."

"I know. I'm just"—I took a deep breath and confessed another truth that I hadn't shared even with Ashton—"I'm afraid I'll never again have what my best friend and my brothers have with their spouses. And the kicker? The kicker is, I'm not even sure I *ever* had it."

No matter how much I'd loved Mason, nor how long, I'd ended up here. Alone on a plane, telling secrets to the window because I was afraid to look at the man I'd just met and tell him that I'd fallen short. That not only had I been wrong but that I'd been so *very* wrong.

The feel of Lucas' gentle fingers under my chin as he turned my head toward him gave me another zing of awareness, followed by the unmistakable knowledge that I was about to cry. I tried for a smile, since it seemed like the right thing to do, but failure soon found me as the first wet tear tracked down my cheek.

Lucas used his thumb to wipe the offending tear away, his index and middle finger still holding me in place, and a mischievous-looking smirk tilting his lips. "Did I mention he's a cunt?"

The words startled me into laughter. Thankfully, I was at least able to keep it low, in deference to the people around us who were starting to settle into quietness.

"You know, you *did* actually mention it," I replied with a smile, aware that another tear was cresting down my cheek. He wiped that one away too, and I reached up to grip his wrist.

It was warm under my touch, and that warmth seemed to transfer into my palm and up my arm. Until this flight—until the first time Lucas had touched me—it had been a wholly unfamiliar sensation, something I'd never experienced with another person.

I liked it. I liked it a lot.

"Thank you," I whispered, trying to say more with those two words than was truly possible. Because he hadn't just wiped away my tears.

He'd listened to my story and hadn't judged me.

He'd taken my side, even though he didn't know me, didn't know if maybe I'd somehow contributed to the failure of my marriage.

And he'd given me a reason to laugh and to smile, even as the old pain took one more shot at my battered heart.

His accent seemed thicker when he said, "No worries," but what did I know? I could've been imagining that, distracted as I was by the charged moment and that warm zingy feeling now creeping its way across my chest. And because, even though I'd just finished recounting my sad story, in that moment I could've sworn his eyes darted down to my lips.

Like he was thinking about kissing me.

"Sir, do you know what you'd like for dinner?" The

friendly voice of the flight attendant cut into our moment, and before I knew it, Lucas was sitting back against his seat, smiling and accepting a tray from the woman who'd interrupted us.

"And for you, ma'am?" She turned her attention to me, and I suddenly understood the saying "like a deer caught in headlights." I had no idea what I wanted to eat, or even what they were serving beyond the fact that there were three choices.

No lie, I was so thrown by the intensity of what had just passed between Lucas and me, I wasn't even sure of my own name.

"Ah, I'm sorry," I apologized with a sheepish smile. *I was too distracted by my handsome as hell seat mate and my depressing back story to look at the options.* "Could you tell me what's available?"

I was so busy paying attention to the flight attendant that I didn't realize Lucas had leaned closer to me once more, and when the low timbre of his voice sounded in my ear, I jumped. "What?" I asked him, quickly glancing up with a mouthed, "Sorry," for the poor woman who probably just wanted to hand me a dinner tray and move on.

"I grabbed the chicken, so if you get the pasta, we can share?"

"Share?" I blinked at him. I couldn't share a meal with him. *Could I?* I'd known him for, what, two hours? Sharing meals was an intimate act. But then again, so was sharing your sordid past, confessing buried secrets and getting lost in a heated, could've-been-a-kiss moment.

"Yeah, come on. Don't tell me you're unfamiliar with the concept. I transfer some of my food to your plate and vice versa, then afterward we can compare notes." Lucas grinned at me and, even though I was totally taken aback—not just by the exchange, but honestly, by most everything since I'd boarded the plane—I grinned back.

Turning to the flight attendant, I requested the pasta with another apology for taking so long, before turning to Lucas. "Thank you."

"For?"

"Not judging me."

"I could definitely be judging you right now, and you wouldn't even know it," he joked.

I wanted to say more, explain that he'd somehow found a way to drag me from under the cloud of the past faster than anyone else had, but instead I copped out. By asking Lucas what he was drinking.

Smooth, Bianca.

"Just water for me." He raised the small plastic cup on his seat tray. "Gotta keep hydrated. Can't be disembarking with cankles, now, can I?"

"Um, I guess not?" I had absolutely no idea how to respond to that. Did men worry about cankles? Or was he joking with me again, like he had with the whole convict thing?

"Lots of fluids, keep stretching your joints, make sure to walk about the cabin every hour or so," he recited with a firm nod.

"Are you a doctor or something?" I asked. "Sorry, excuse me." I reached past him to accept my tray from the flight attendant, then turned back to Lucas. "Or do you write health and safety pamphlets for a living? You seem well-versed in flight safety."

He peeled back the aluminum cover of his meal. "Nope, not a doctor. Or a"—he paused, that mischievous look back on his face—"*pamphlet* writer. I just happen to be generally brilliant."

"This from the man who was worried he wasn't 'wowing' me with his brains?"

"Self-deprecating humor. Trust me, if you're looking for brilliance, you'll find it right here." He pointed to himself with his plastic airplane fork.

"Modesty too?" I asked, not even trying to hide the mockery in my tone.

"Obviously."

"So, tell me, Mister Generally Brilliant, what is it you do?" I asked, figuring it was probably high time we talked about something other than me. Peeling back the cover on my own meal, I stared down at the unappetizing looking pasta. "You know, I'm not so sure pasta was a good idea."

"Nah, it's okay. I had it on the way over. It tastes better than it looks, promise." This time, he used the fork in his hand to point down at the chicken on his tray. "Hoping the same is true here."

Inspecting his meal, I frowned. It really didn't look any better than my pasta. "I'm not sure I'd trust that."

"You said you'd share with me, so you're about to find out."

My mouth fell open. "I never actually agreed," I countered, narrowing my eyes at him in a way I hoped he'd recognize as playful. I wasn't really averse to sharing with him, you see, but I loved the way talking shit with and to him made me feel: light-hearted in a way I could barely remember being.

"Oh, bugger that. You all but agreed when you ordered the pasta." As if to illustrate his stance, he reached out and speared one of the spirals, popping it into his mouth with a triumphant expression. "Mm, good."

"Hey! You said you'd already had it, so if you wanted it, you should've ordered it. It's mine now." I placed my arm on the side of my tray table and leaned forward a little, making like I was protecting my food from him. "You snooze, you lose."

He widened his eyes and opened his now-empty mouth in—I assumed—faux-shock. "You're reneging! You're a reneger!"

"I am not. You can't renege when you never agreed in the first place." I poked my tongue out at him, laughing when he pretended to poke at it with his fork. "Quit it."

Wrinkling his nose, he turned back to his meal, muttering what sounded suspiciously like "reneger" under his breath.

"You'd better watch your mouth, buddy." I was just about to poke him in the side—with my finger or my own fork, I hadn't yet decided—when the full weight of the craziness of our exchange and my behavior struck me.

I'd gone from crying over my past to sharing a meal and a stupid laugh with this man I didn't know.

Not to mention what was very possibly a near-kiss moment.

It was insanity, and yet . . . it hadn't felt like it as it happened. All of it—the conversation, the bantering, the goddamn zinging. It felt as natural, more so, than anything that had happened with Mason when we'd first met. Back when we were still barely adults and just becoming friends who'd someday grow into something more.

Then something less.

"When did you stop loving me?"

I'd asked him that, sometime after it'd all fallen apart, and he'd sought me out to "explain." Only I'd never gotten an answer from him. Just stony silence as we discussed the division of assets, and a wealth of doubts when it was all said and done.

The glimmer of excitement I felt about how I'd reacted to Lucas—how easily I'd fallen into talking to him, teasing him and nearly kissing him—warred with the protective instinct that had grown around me in the wake of Mason.

The one that this whole trip was supposed to help me overcome, damn it.

It curdled in my stomach and made me want to withdraw, but the excitement? It was still there, lingering under the surface and still fighting to be let back out, so I focused on it. I gripped it with both hands to stop it from drowning altogether.

"You okay?" Lucas nudged me with his elbow. "We don't really have to share if you don't want to."

I considered his question. *Am I okay?* I took careful stock of my body, considered the effect his voice and the way he could switch from fun to caring had on me, and smiled. Because in the tight grip of my hands, the excitement was winning the war.

And I suddenly had a big, bold, probably stupid question that I really wanted the answer to. "If she hadn't interrupted us, would you have kissed me?"

5

LUCAS

Bugger me, this woman was beautiful. The riot of ebony curls, her eyes dark brown and her lips—killer. Lush, plump and . . . was she really asking me if I'd have kissed her? Because the answer to that was simple.

"Yes." Okay, so maybe the answer was more like *hell yes,* but I figured it was better not to go too overboard. I was all for honesty—and how could I not give her that when she'd asked so boldly if I'd had her lips on my mind?—but I didn't want to scare her off.

My answer made her face light up with a slow smile. Like it took the one word response a moment or two to sink in. And Jesus fucking Christ, I liked the way she looked at me, happiness in those eyes and on that mouth.

Especially after hearing the story of how her dickhead husband had become her dickhead *ex*-husband.

"Good to know." She dipped her head in a shy nod, and I wondered if I needed to wait for another moment like the one we'd just shared. Or could I just lean in and kiss her like I so badly wanted to?

I was still trying to decide on that when she laid a hand

on my arm. I want to say that it was nothing—just a light touch to get my attention—but that'd be a lie. I felt that touch not just in my forearm but everywhere.

Especially my cock.

What? I said I was all for honesty.

"You know it's your turn to tell me about you, right?" She raised her eyebrows as if she expected me to protest. Not happening. I wanted her to know me as badly as I wanted to know her. The way I figured it, we had a dozen or so hours left to get to know one another, before we went our separate ways.

But twelve hours arm-to-arm, thigh-to-thigh in economy class on a crowded aeroplane counted extra in the getting-to-know-you stakes. Surely by the end of the flight, she'd know if she wanted to see me again.

"What do you want to know, pretty girl?" I asked, placing my hand over hers on my forearm. I couldn't resist the urge to run a finger over the back of her hand, the mocha skin warm and soft, the caress sending another whiff of lavender into the air. "Middle name? Height? University degree?"

"Sure," she said through a laugh, "we can start there."

"Righto, so"—I paused for a sec, realizing I shouldn't have offered my middle name up for the taking and hoping she didn't notice if I side-stepped it—"I'm a hundred eighty-six centimeters, which is six-one-ish. And I studied Human Movement, at least initially." I didn't mention that I'd gone back to school and graduated with a doctorate in Health Sciences, in the hopes she'd hear the "initially" and ask more questions.

It was a bloody brilliant plan that didn't take into account one little thing—she could apparently read me like a book and knew I was trying to hide something from her.

"And your middle name?" The way she tilted her head

told me she'd realized I'd left it out, while the arched eyebrow and cheeky look in her eye said she suspected I'd done so on purpose. "Don't forget that."

Relinquishing her hand, I shoveled some chicken into my mouth, chewing and swallowing before offering my opinion. "Not bad, actually. Offer's still open if you wanna taste."

"I'll pass, but thanks." She turned back to her own meal and I breathed a sigh of relief. *Crisis averted.* Only I'd once again underestimated her, and wasn't that just the stupidest thing ever?

"You weren't wrong about the pasta." She grabbed the serviette from the packet of utensils that came with the meal and wiped around her mouth. "And your middle name is?"

She so casually added it, that I nearly answered. Catching myself at the last minute, I asked, "So, about that kiss?" With my lips puckered as if ready to meet hers, I leaned in closer, making her giggle as she leaned back the same amount, using the serviette to cover her mouth.

"Nuh-uh, I want to know now. It must be bad if you're trying to avoid telling me."

I gave her a pout that was both very real—I wanted to kiss her so badly—and exaggerated so she'd know I wasn't a total leering arse, leaned back and shrugged. "It's nothing. It's-I mean, I don't have one?"

"Are you asking me or telling me you don't have one? Because I'd say you do, and now I'm wondering if there's a way to find out without you telling me . . ." She trailed off and began tap, tap, tapping on her lips, which reminded me of the nervous way she'd tapped her passport against her hand in the terminal.

Which in turn reminded me that I felt more in tune with this woman in the two-ish hours we'd been seatmates than I had with most of my ex-girlfriends. Combined. Something about the ease with which we'd connected—it felt different. It felt like more.

"Is this a nervous habit of yours? The tapping thing?" I asked out of a need to avoid her question but also a need to know.

"What tapping thing?" She narrowed her gaze on me and I felt seen. Like, fully exposed. But then, as if realizing my game, her eyes flicked to the seat in front of her. And when she met my eyes again, a devilish grin tilted her mouth.

It only made her more beautiful. *Shit.* Still, what answer could the seatback entertainment and/or her nearly-empty dinner tray have given her? She clearly thought she'd come up with something.

"I have an idea." She wiggled her eyebrows and reached out to tap, tap, tap on my arm. "A way to find out."

"If you're a nervous tapper, you mean?"

"Ha, nice try. I know I am. Though I am impressed by your observation skills. I'll add it to your list of attributes along with brilliance and modesty."

"I saw you in the terminal," I confessed. I could've just told her my middle name—though I wasn't exactly hyped at the idea—but I was enjoying myself too much to give in. And a part of me wanted her to know that I'd seen her. I noticed her.

Ignoring my confession, she kept talking, "I think mayyyyybe I'll wait until you fall asleep, then dig out your passport." Lifting those tapping fingers in front of her mouth, she made out like she was shocked she'd suggested it.

She wasn't.

But, thankfully, I had an ace in the hole. Because there

was a fatal flaw with her plan: there was *no way* I was falling asleep when she was sitting next to me and I only had limited time to get to know her.

Still, I played along. "You're diabolical."

"If you didn't want to tell me, you shouldn't have offered the information in the first place. And you called *me* a reneger." She shook her head, sadness in her movement. "You kind of suck, Lucas *Archibald*—I just realized I don't know your last name either."

"That I don't mind sharing. Hawke. With an 'E'. And I hate to break it to you, but you won't guess my middle name."

Eyes narrowing in challenge, she said, "Lucas Francisco Hawke has a nice ring to it."

Shaking my head, I replied, "Nope, sorry. Hey, what's *your* surname?"

"Evers. But don't think you're going to distract me."

"You're saying you won't Evers be distracted?"

She glared at me, looking not at all impressed by my play on her last name, though I knew it was just an act. "Hilarious. Okay, Lucas Norbert? No, that's not it. Lucas Winthrop Hawke. The Fourth."

"The fourth? That's a nice touch, but no. Sorry."

"It's funny, you know. My friend's husband is a 'fourth,' and my friend once had to try and guess his name too."

"Ah, but I'm not a fourth. Maybe later you can tell me that story, though."

"Maybe," she replied, with a sigh and a pout. It was so bloody cute, I nearly spilled the beans, but I was having too much fun to cave just then. "Fine, Lucas Herbert Hawke. Alliteration is Awesome, After All." Emphasizing the 'A' in each word, she laughed at her own joke, and I couldn't help but smile with her. Meanwhile, the man in the seat next to me made a small noise, and I turned to see him watching us.

"You okay, mate?" I asked, not wanting to be rude, but wanting to make sure he wasn't a) going to try to participate in this game between me and *my* pretty seatmate, and b) complain or some shit, and ruin the fun.

"Yeah, sorry. Didn't mean to interrupt, but Herbert made me think of Herbie. You know, the old bug car?" He looked sheepish. "Couldn't help but laugh at the idea of someone liking that old show enough to name their kid after it."

I was about to say something in reply, when Bianca leaned forward to look around me, and stole both of our attention. "I loved that show. Probably not enough to name my kid after it, but yeah, don't mock the bug."

Giving her a wide smile, probably because being included by her made his whole damn year—I know talking to her was making mine—he nodded. "My apologies."

"You're forgiven."

With another nod, he started fumbling with the airline-provided headphones, while Bianca leaned back in her seat. "You need to just tell me." Another sigh, this one exasperated. "We don't have all day."

"On the contrary," I began, before she was pressing her fingers to my lips to silence me.

"Nope, no more excuses and no more trying to get out of telling me." She started to pull her hand away but seeing as how I liked her fingers on me, and I wasn't ready for the contact to break, I quickly circled her wrist with my hand, holding her in place. "I'll make you a deal," she offered.

I raised my eyebrows to let her know I was listening then, because I couldn't resist the urge, I puckered my lips to give her fingers a small, soft kiss.

A blush formed on her cheeks, and she lowered her

voice, leaning in. "If you tell me your middle name, I'll give you that kiss we missed earlier."

Deal. I wanted to yell my middle name at her and get to the kissing, but instead, I nodded, then used my hold on her wrist to lift her palm to my lips. Brushing my lips across it, I released her, feeling like a fucking champion when she brought her hand to rest on my neck instead of letting it drop away.

Leaning in, until my lips were barely a whisper from hers, and I could feel her warm breath start to come quicker and quicker, I murmured, "Valentine."

And then, I kissed her.

6

BIANCA

Don't stop.

Please, don't ever *stop.*

Lucas' lips were warm and soft and so perfect, it was all I could do to not climb into his lap and press him for more.

More. More. More.

God, the way he kissed me and the way he moved his hands so he was gently cupping the sides of my neck was . . .

Everything.

His kiss was everything.

It was the ease with which I'd talked to him. The way he'd made me spill my secrets. The fact that, with him, I could forget the hurt I'd just dredged up to laugh and flirt instead.

His kiss was the zing I'd felt every time we'd touched—no matter how innocent—amplified to the *nth* degree. It zipped up and down my body, along every nerve-ending, until it short-circuited my brain. Until my thoughts became fragmented, broken pleas for him to kiss me longer.

To kiss me always.

And even though I knew it was insane, it was also so

goddamn right, I didn't have a hope of pulling back. Until he chose to stop it, I was going to kiss him and kiss him and kiss him some more.

It's never been like this. An obsession—that was the only word for it. From the moment our lips touched, I was obsessed with his kiss, with him.

With his lips, and how they moved and danced and guided mine.

With his tongue, and the way it swept into my mouth, tasting me and letting me taste him in return.

With the low rumble that started in his chest and felt like it was vibrating through my body, centering in on that spot between my legs that ached.

God, *god,* how it ached.

I lifted my hand so it rested on his side, the thin material of his T-shirt no barrier against the heat emanating from him. I could feel his muscles as they stretched and moved under his skin, and I wanted to see them too. Bare and moving because he was moving with me. Over me. Under me. Next to me. Around me.

Inside me.

I want him.

I wanted space—not from him, but for us. So I could push him back, or so he could push me back. So we could stretch out together and turn this kiss into something that involved our whole bodies.

I wanted . . .

I just *wanted.* In a way I'd never wanted before.

And all because of his kiss.

"Bianca," he whispered, pulling his lips back only enough that he could say my name like it was a prayer. "Bianca."

I nodded, knowing—somehow just knowing—that he

was asking for permission to kiss me again. Kiss me more. And even though I'd already granted it, it didn't stop me from pleading with him, my voice holding a note of desperation I didn't, couldn't, even try to hide.

"Please. *Please,* Lucas."

Our mouths clashed again as we both moved to close that minute space between us, and everything else dropped away. The hum of the airplane as it barreled through the clouds, the near-silent buzz that hung in the air, the tidy movements of the flight attendants as they moved about the cabin clearing the dinner trays. All of it, gone.

Lost because all I could think about and feel and wish for and want was Lucas. And his kiss.

Feeling my hand fist in his shirt, the bunching of cotton under my palm, I realized that I was gripping him so tightly, it was like my body had decided that it was never letting go. And even though I knew that was silly, it didn't *feel* silly.

It felt like tingles and sparks and little electric pulses bringing my nerves to life.

It felt like slick heat and a rush of wetness readying my body for him.

It felt like the pounding of my heart against my rib cage.

It felt . . . right.

I know what you're thinking, because if I hadn't felt it myself, if I hadn't experienced the utter and complete rightness of that kiss, I'd have thought the same.

Impossible.

I didn't know him. He didn't even qualify as a passing acquaintance because that would imply that I'd met him sometime before; that before we'd found ourselves side-by-side on a long-haul flight to Australia, we'd come across each other in some small way.

But I knew this kiss. I knew it was designed for me and me alone.

I knew that it was nothing like how Mason had kissed me, even in the beginning. It was better.

That scared the shit out of me. Because I'd loved Mason. Loved kissing him. Loved the way he'd held me and touched me.

Loved it enough to marry him. And he'd betrayed me.

Echoes of pain lanced my heart, a flash flood of memories crashing in and sweeping me away.

"I love you, B. I love you."

"I need you with me always."

"There'll never be anyone but you."

"She . . . she gave me what I needed. And you didn't. Wouldn't."

"You're so angry at me, when you should be angry with yourself."

With Mason's voice in my head, reminding me of the good and the bad, dragging me out of the undertow, I did the only thing I could.

I unclenched my hand, difficult as it was.

I drew back, hating the way Lucas' lips tried to follow mine.

I turned away, my back hitting my seat, sending a jolt of awareness through me.

We were on a plane, surrounded by hundreds of other passengers, and we'd been shamelessly making out. I don't know how it looked to the people around us, but my imaginings didn't paint the prettiest of pictures.

Biting my lower lip, I turned slowly to look at Lucas, because I needed to know what he was thinking. As if I could tell just by looking at him.

With flushed cheeks and a mouth slightly ajar, he

looked . . . stunned. When his eyes met mine after what could've been two seconds or twenty, they were filled with questions.

What was that?

Did you feel it too?

Why did you stop?

Can I kiss you again?

Do you regret it?

It was the last one that worried me most, because I didn't know the answer. I wanted to say no, that I didn't regret it at all. But I didn't want to lie. Not to myself. Not to him.

Sucking in a deep breath, I opened my mouth because I knew I needed to say something. To explain why I pulled back or tease him about his middle name or . . . or . . . or . . .

Something, Bianca. Say something.

Running sentence after sentence after sentence in my mind didn't give me a clear idea of what the right move or the right words were, and the longer I took to talk, the more I felt the awkwardness of the moment build.

I didn't want it to be awkward. I didn't want to take something that had been *everything* for a heartbeat or five and taint it even more than the memory of Mason and his betrayal had, so I did the only thing I could.

Checking to see if the seatbelt sign had come on during our kiss—the plane could have plummeted from the sky, and I don't think I'd have noticed—I unbuckled my belt and looked at Lucas with pleading eyes, the memory of how I'd said "*please*" sparking back to life.

And then, I made a play for more time. "I need to get up."

He looked down at the dinner trays still in front of us and helplessly back at me. "You might have to—"

I was shaking my head, refusing to acknowledge what he

was saying, before he'd even finished saying it. "I have to get up."

"Okay. Um, just, hold on." He grabbed my tray and slid it over to his own and I quickly lifted my tray table back up, locking it in place. Staring down at my hands instead of at Lucas, I heard him asking the man in the aisle seat if he would mind getting up. "Bianca?"

"Thank you." I stood and eased my way across the seats, more grateful than I could say that they'd managed to get up and out of my way while holding the debris of dinner. I opened my mouth to say something else, but nothing came out. Instead I just turned and moved down the aisle, drawing a couple of odd looks from the passengers around us who obviously knew something was going on, and made my way to the back of the plane with most of my sanity still intact. But the moment I closed the bathroom door behind me, I dropped down onto the closed toilet lid and shuddered out a sob.

Why? Why did he have—still have—so much power over me?

All I could think was that I was somehow broken, and I didn't want to think it. Accept it. Or believe it. Because Mason didn't deserve that kind of power over me—not ever, but certainly not anymore.

"It was not your fault. You didn't make him cheat." I was talking to myself, but something about hearing the words aloud helped. "Don't let his voice be the one inside your head. Don't let him take anything else from you." I nodded at that last one, reminding myself that I couldn't control him—not that I'd want to—but I could control my reaction to him and the choices he'd made. And even if it was nothing more than his voice in my head, only *I* could decide how to react to it.

Standing, I turned slightly to look at myself in the mirror and found that I liked what I saw. Here was a woman who'd tried and failed but who hadn't given up. "Well, you've haven't *completely* given up," I told my reflection, knowing that I'd had my moments, "and that's a good start."

That Bianca looking back at me, she was a woman who'd been hurt but who was recovering. A woman who'd been thrown over but who was becoming stronger. A woman who'd kissed a veritable stranger on an airplane and enjoyed it.

At least until the past had crept in and tainted it. But hell, if Rome wasn't built in a day, then neither could I be. I just had to remember to be kinder to myself, and that this trip was about taking chances and learning new things and shaping the person I'd become *A.M.*—after marriage.

And if it also became a little bit about kissing a hot guy, then so be it.

7

LUCAS

"You going to go after her?"

"Huh?" I forced myself to stop watching Bianca as she made her way down the aisle, clearly heading for the back of the plane and the toilets. Turning to look at the man who shared our row, I found that he'd already sat back in his aisle seat, dropped his tray table down and put his dinner rubbish back on it.

He'd actually made it so I couldn't sit down without asking him to move. Again.

I have to get up. She'd looked so . . . broken when she'd made that request, there was no way I could deny her. Tray tables and plastic cutlery be damned.

"You're going after her, right?" The man spoke again, his voice quiet but all the more compelling for it. "You need to be there when she gets out of the bathroom, man."

I thought about that, wondered if he was right. Would that scare her? I opened my mouth to ask him, when he spoke again.

"Take it from a man who's been married for a few years now"—he looked down at the ring on his left hand, a small smile forming—"she needs you. But not to press her for more. Just be there, so she's not alone."

I nodded slowly. He made sense—I could be there to make sure she was okay, without expecting anything from her. I mean, I was still reeling from that kiss too.

That kiss.

Fuck, but it had been the single most intense experience of my life.

Holding out my hand, I said, "Thanks, man. 'Preciate it."

He took it, shaking firmly. "Good luck, Lucas."

Dropping his hand—and letting my eyes widen in question—I asked, "You know my name?"

"I can't help but overhear you two, you know," he replied with a laugh. "Seems like there's something good happening."

Remembering the way he'd first said, "Jesus," then later joked about Herbie the Love Bug, I laughed with him, a new opinion forming of the man who'd interrupted us. "Right. Sorry about that."

He shrugged. "No big deal. You don't have smelly feet, you're not trimming your nails or eating a can of tuna, and you're not crowding me, so I can handle being on the sidelines of flirting." His smile was that of a man who'd had some terrible flying experiences. "I'm Anton. And you'd better get a move on, man."

My eyes darted down the aisle, Bianca now nowhere in sight. "Thanks, Anton."

His nod was shallow, the acceptance of my gratitude obvious, and then I was moving carefully down the small aisle, trying to avoid overhanging elbows or legs stretched out in the hunt for a few extra centimeters of room. The cabin was starting to get quieter, though this part of the plane had yet to be cleared of dinner debris, and I wondered what these passengers had thought when Bianca had passed by.

Had they been paying attention to the gorgeous woman with sad eyes? Because they should've been, and I had a feeling they hadn't. That they, like her cockweasel of an ex, hadn't *seen* her.

Not the way I saw her.

When I got to the galley at the back of the plane, I found it empty and all bathrooms free, except for one. So that's the one I watched, waiting for my skittish seatmate to appear.

It took several minutes—and a little bit of inaudible murmuring from inside the toilet—but when the red "occupied" light turned to green, I stood a little straighter. Bianca didn't make an appearance right away, and I figured it was because she still needed time. And that, I could give her.

My sister had always called me a hopeless romantic, and despite all the times I'd thought I'd found something special, they'd never compared to this. This brief, wild connection with Bianca. Instinct was telling me that I needed to be patient with her; we had potential and a real chance at something good, as long as I didn't rush it.

But Jesus Christ, after that kiss, rushing it was so damn tempting.

The door folded open, and there she was. Beautiful and a little subdued. She was looking down, and I didn't want her to startle when she stepped out of the tiny space and into me, so I started simply. "Hey, pretty girl."

Her head whipped up and her eyes told me that she was torn between relief at seeing me and worry for what I might be about to ask of her. "I just wanted to make sure you were okay." I held my hands up, the worldwide gesture for "no harm meant here," and offered a small smile. "And I wanted to say I'm sorry."

Her forehead wrinkled in a frown, and she blinked a couple of times before opening her mouth to respond, but I cut her off before she could. Because I didn't want there to be any confusion. "I'm not sorry for kissing you. You made me an offer I couldn't refuse, and I'd do it again in a heartbeat. But I am sorry you're hurting, and I'm sorry if I made it worse. But, yeah, please don't ask me to regret kissing you."

I will never regret kissing you. It was a whisper from something inside me—the hopeless romantic part, I suppose.

Her response was to step toward me, and my heart pounded at her closeness. If I wanted, I could reach out and haul her into my arms. It was tempting as hell, so I shoved my hands into the pockets of my trackies to avoid temptation. The grey material shifted, the waistband pulling down slightly, and I watched Bianca's eyes fall.

She was checking me out again and it was all I could do to not rip my hand from my pocket and execute a fist pump. But again, I was trying not to rush while also trying to maintain a cool exterior. Back to that whole *don't let on that you're an idiot and an arsehole too early* thing.

"Lucas?" It took a minute, maybe two, for her to finally speak, but when she did, I was ready.

"Bianca?"

She smiled at me, her eyes roaming up my body until our eyes met. "I'm not sorry we kissed either."

Yes. I was still a mere heartbeat away from that fist pump, when she spoke again.

"Will you tell me a little bit more about you?" Her voice was soft with a thread of need in it. She wanted, I thought, for me to level the playing field, which was confirmed by her next words. "I feel like . . . I don't know, like I've laid myself bare. And I'd kind of like to know more about you so it doesn't feel quite so one-sided." Her frown reappeared and she mouthed something to herself that I didn't understand. "It's not just that though. I like you and I'd like to know more about you. More than just your height and education."

"Confession: you don't even know the extent of my education."

"You're holding out on me?"

"A little, but in my own defense, I was trying to distract you."

"Because Valentine, huh?"

"Exactly."

She laughed, her frown giving way to barely-there lines of happiness. "So, will you?"

"Tell you more about myself? Sure." I understood that me knowing her story gave me an advantage and it seemed like a no-brainer to agree. Plus, I was just relieved she was still interested. I don't know what I'd have done if she walked out of that toilet saying she wanted nothing to do with me.

Nothing too serious though. You never know when there's an air marshall on board.

Leaning back against the wall of the plane at the place where it bulged out to make a kind of bench, I gave her carte blanche to ask what she would. "What do you want to know?"

Her mouth curved. "Why Valentine?"

I rolled my eyes at her. Of course she'd take that nugget of information and press for more. "My dad loved the book *Stranger in a Strange Land.* Apparently, he was big into Sci-Fi."

"Was?"

"He died when I was two. I don't remember anything, except what Mum's told me about him." The same feeling I always got when I thought about my dad crept in, and I frowned. "She gives me a new photo of him every year on his birthday."

I'd never told anyone outside of my immediate family about that. And yet, it was natural to let Bianca in on the secret.

"I love that. But I'm sorry about your dad."

I didn't know how to accept her condolences, so instead I shared one of the photos with her, as best I could without it in front of me. "I have a photo of them on their wedding day. Mum gave it to me when I turned eighteen."

"It's your favorite."

See? She got it and me. "Yeah, it is." I gestured to her. "Come here, I'll show you."

"You have it with you?" she asked even as she followed instructions and came within reach.

"No, but . . ." I wrapped an arm around her waist and waited to see if she'd tell me to let go or stop touching her. She didn't. "He's holding her like this," I explained, bringing my other arm up to rest on her chest, just above her heart. "And laughing. She's smiling at him like I don't know what. I asked her what he'd said or done right before the picture, but she just looked away."

Bianca's eyes softened. "And was she holding him back? Too, I mean."

"I knew what you meant. And yes. She had her hands on his hips."

"Like this?" Her hand rested softly on my sides, and I felt like I'd been branded. "Lucas?"

I shook myself, not realizing that I'd lost the thread of what we were talking about. "Sorry. Like that, yes."

"Maybe he was telling her that her heart was his, and that his belonged to her."

"Maybe."

"Or maybe he was just reassuring himself that she was real."

I swallowed roughly, Bianca's romantic thoughts making me think about what it must've felt like for my dad to hold his heart in his arms. Feeling exposed, I played it off. "Or he was trying to cop a feel and noticed the wedding photographer just in time."

Bianca wrinkled her nose and took a step away from me, making my arms fall away from her body and leaving my sides feeling colder. "I don't think so. And I don't think you do either."

I felt like an arsehole for taking the moment and ruining it, but I couldn't help it.

She might have exposed herself and her past to me, but I was this close to exposing my present to her—the fact that I knew something about us was important—and I was fucking afraid to risk her saying no. To hear her say she couldn't or didn't want to.

She had baggage, I knew that. She'd just hauled it out of her seat, down the aisle and into the bathroom. But so did I.

After a silence that hit just this side of awkward, her head tilted in question. "Did your mum ever get remarried or anything?"

Nodding, I brushed away thoughts of rejection and thought instead of my stepdad, James. Although I'd always known he wasn't my biological dad, I'd never thought of him as anything but "Dad." He was the man who raised me, who taught me what I needed to know, who loved my mum so much that I knew I wouldn't ever settle for anything less than that. That kind of connection.

The kind of connection I thought I saw everywhere but hadn't really, honestly felt until I'd sat down next to Bianca. Shaking away the thought once more, because I didn't want to betray it too soon and scare Bianca—or hell, *myself*—away, I kept talking. "Mum met James when I was . . . three? Ish? He always said he knew she was the one from the moment she placed an order for a Happy Meal in front of him."

"At McDonald's? They met at McDonald's?" Disbelief colored Bianca's voice and her face and I laughed. Because, yeah, it wasn't like Macca's was the hub of meet-cutes for singles.

"Hey, settle down. Mum was raising me alone and I loved Macca's. Still do, to be honest."

"Macca's?" Her accompanying giggle was soft and adorable, and my mind flashed back to our kiss and the way she'd gripped my shirt. The cotton still held the faint wrinkles her fist had put there.

"Pro tip about us Aussies: we abbreviate a lot."

She nodded. "Got it." Moving to lean against the bench formed by the aeroplane wall beside me, she added, "Continue, please."

"So, Mum orders me a Happy Meal and herself a Big Mac meal—her favorite back then, though she doesn't eat them anymore—and goes to pay, but she only has a fiver. No card or anything, just a five dollar note and some small change."

"Did James pay?" She turned her head so she was watching me and her eyes widened a fraction. "Please tell me he did." She was invested in my story and I reveled in it. Because it made the worry that had lingered disappear.

"Of course. On the proviso she ate with him." I shook my head at the memory of Dad telling the story of how he fell in love with her after he watched her deconstruct the final bite of her burger. "She used to eat her Big Mac weird. The last bite or two, she'd take apart and eat the buns first, then the meat. Apparently, that's what did it for him."

"Do you remember it happening?"

Shaking my head, I replied, "I was probably in the play area for most of it. In fact, I know I was because that's what they told me. My first real memory is of Dad—James—helping me make breakfast in bed for Mum on . . . Mother's Day, maybe? I knocked over the vase with the flowers we'd picked from the garden and cried. He told me she'd love her pancake anyway, even if it was soggy. And he was right."

"He sounds like a good man."

"He's the best man. I miss my bio dad because I never knew him and because I know he loved me. Mum made sure I knew that. But I never felt like I missed out on anything because I had, I *have,* a dad who loves me."

She made a small noise of happiness as her hand brushed across mine tentatively. Looking down to see if it was a mistake or an invitation, I carefully wrapped my hand around hers and linked our fingers.

Invitation.

Looking back up to smile at her before giving her a little more of my story, I added, "They got married when I was five. I was the best man. And then they had Rose, my baby sister."

Bianca's hand tightened in mine. "Your voice changed just now. Is—is Rose okay?"

"I think so, now. She's had a rough few years, but she's doing better. At least, that's what both she and Mum have told me. I'll get to see her for Christmas this year, so I'll be able to judge for myself."

"You missed last Christmas?"

"No, she did. She's been living in North Carolina for a couple of years for work."

Her hand tightened against mine. "Really?"

"Yeah, why?"

"Um, because that's where my family is from." Her full lips pursed, then tilted up at the corners. A small smile that made me want to lean in and brush my lips over hers. "My parents and brothers still live there."

"Small world." Not that small, of course, but there was no doubting the fact that it was a coincidence that made whatever was happening seem even more important.

"So, you didn't visit her during your trip? I mean, you weren't in the States to see her or whatever?"

I shook my head, wanting to sigh at my stupidity while also being grateful that my hopeless romantic tendencies had put me on a plane to the USA, not to visit my sister, but in pursuit of a girl. A girl, it turned out, who wasn't for me.

Because now I was talking to a girl that *was* for me. Somehow, I knew it. No deconstructed Big Mac required.

"Then why?" Bianca asked, her curiosity obvious.

Rolling my eyes, I said in my best self-deprecating voice, "Because I'm an idiot. And because of a girl named Erin."

"Erin, huh? I'm going to need to know more about this Erin."

"Yeah." I shook my head at my remembered stupidity and thought about where to begin. But first I asked, "You want a snack? We can make it a picnic back here."

Bianca's eyebrows furrowed. "What do you mean?"

Pointing at the small kitchen-type area in the galley, I said, "This is why I love flying my nation's airline. Free drinks and snacks." With her hand still in mine, I moved closer to the food. "See?"

"They have . . ." She trailed off, looking at the small fridges that held soft drinks and little bottles of water and the baskets filled with muesli bites and Tim Tams. "This is awesome."

After reluctantly letting go of her hand, I opened one of the fridges, and grabbed a Coke. Holding it out to her, I raised my eyebrows in question. She smiled and took it, and after grabbing myself a can, I looked over the rest of the offerings. "Whatcha think? Tim Tams get my vote."

"I've never had one." She shrugged, but it was obvious from the gleam in her eye she wanted it. The biscuit, that is. I could only hope she wanted something else, if you know what I mean. "I'm going to Australia to push myself and try new things so . . . yes?"

"I think you mean *hell yes*, pretty girl."

She laughed, as intended, and I made a point of grabbing four of the little packets. "I think this should be enough, but let's stay close by, just in case. Reckon we could get away with sitting back here?"

She looked about, same as me, and obviously decided that the two people at the other end of the small hall-type area weren't going to be an issue, because she nodded. "Will the flight attendants come back here?"

"I don't think so. I'm pretty sure the galley where they prepare all the meals and get rid of stuff is back that way." I pointed down the plane. "This is just the small snack area, and it's mostly bathrooms"—I gestured to the different toilets located nearby—"and since the plane is mostly sleeping, it's going to be pretty private."

Nodding again, she moved to the least-intrusive place and sat cross-legged on the floor. Though there wasn't a lot of room, it didn't seem to bother her and it sure as hell didn't bother me. I was just glad that she'd agreed to spend more time with me.

"This floor is probably filthy." Her nose scrunched up

and I had the unmistakable urge to kiss it. And then her forehead.

I dunno. It just seemed like the kind of thing we'd both enjoy.

"Probably," I agreed, sitting next to her and handing her a packet of Tim Tams. There were two in each, so I asked, "Should we share? You know, in the unlikely event you don't like the biscuit of my people?"

Nodding, she ripped open the packet and handed me one before taking the other and inspecting it. "It *looks* delicious. But looks can be deceiving."

"Yes, because I also look delicious and—" I wasn't really sure where I was going with that sentence—I'd started saying it before I'd consciously thought about it—but thankfully, she interrupted me before I had to figure it out.

"You are delicious." Her teeth caught her lower lip as her eyes darted away, and although the low light in the plane meant that I couldn't see her properly, I had the distinct impression that she was blushing.

But that's okay, because, fuck, so was I.

Don't tell me you wouldn't do the same if a beautiful woman called you delicious.

I leaned in close, bringing my lips close to her ear since her head was still slightly turned away, and whispered, "So are you," then moved back immediately. I didn't want to crowd her, but I also didn't want her thinking she was alone in this *thing* between us either. Although, at this point, how she could have any doubt was a little bit beyond me.

She turned back around, but didn't look at me right away, and that was okay. I was cool with waiting, since we were getting back on the right footing after our kiss derailed us a little.

Okay, that's not completely true, because when she lifted

the Tim Tam to her mouth and nibbled at the corner, cool was the furthest thing from what I was feeling. I was hot. And Bianca? She was *fucking* hot.

The happy moan she gave after that first bite was the death knell for my coolness. I was suddenly trying to hide a rapidly growing boner while also trying to remain impassive. It might've worked, but for the fact my voice broke when I asked, "Liked it, huh?"

Her eyes finally caught mine again and she nodded, her lips curved in a satisfied smile. "Oh, my god. It's so good." Then, in what should've been the least sexy move ever, she shoved the rest of the chocolate biscuit in her mouth and grinned at me.

I was a *goner*.

"You're perfect," I moaned, shifting in what I hoped was a surreptitious manner to relieve the building pressure in my pants. Only the fact I was wearing trackie daks saved me —thank Christ for loose cotton and elastic waistbands.

I thought maybe she'd noticed my . . . pre-DICK-ament when her eyes fell to my lap, but instead of bringing it up—pun intended—she instead said the magic words to make my cock deflate faster than Tom Brady's footballs. "So, tell me about this Erin?"

I silently cursed and praised the gods that be for that segue back to the topic we'd been on before our impromptu picnic. "She was my girlfriend. For about"—I rocked my hand—"three minutes when I decided that following her to the States for a cross-country adventure was a good idea."

Bianca's laugh was startled. "Really?"

Nodding, I explained, "My sister, Rose, has always said I'm a hopeless romantic, and she's not wrong. It's just . . . my mum loved my bio dad, and she loves Dad—James—too. Both men, she told me, she knew right away were the 'one' for her. I want that. And I know that's not necessarily the norm, but there you have it."

"I think it's sweet." She smiled at me and I cringed. Dramatically. And clutched my chest, because I thought it would amuse her and I wanted to amuse her. I wanted to make her think about me and go, "Yeah, he's a good one. I want to see him again." Sue me.

"*Anyway*," I emphasized, "I met Erin at a party some friends were having, and we hit it off. She was beautiful and fun, and I liked her. A lot. And when she said she was planning this trip, I kinda thought, why not? It sounded fun. Rose lives in North Carolina, and since Erin was considering it as one of her stops, I could see my sister, see the States, hang out with my girl." I shrugged again. "I took the time off work—three months, which I'd been saving up for years—and booked my flights."

Bianca's eyes widened, as if she could sense the sad end to my story. Not that it was actually that sad. "Turns out, you don't really know someone until you've travelled with them. Erin was still nice and all, but . . . she was a handful. She'd never say what she wanted to do, then get shitty when I made plans for us that she didn't like. She spent most of her time on her phone, texting friends or whatever instead of experiencing the moment. I don't know." I shrugged again, because it just seemed like the right move. My feelings toward Erin were very *meh* at that point. "I'm sure it would've been fun for someone, but I wanted to explore. See the country. Visit random places and meet people and make the most of it, ya know?"

She nodded, and I could tell understood when she laid her hand on my forearm. I didn't need her words, but she gave them anyway and it felt good. "You just had different priorities for your trip, is all. It's not wrong to want to get your money's worth, so to speak."

"No, I know. I mean, I knew this trip wouldn't be one I could do again, at least not for ages. So, when she announced in Texas that she'd met someone—a cowboy, of course, you know, *Texas*—"

Bianca cut me off with a laugh, her hand tightening on my arm. It sent a wave of heat through me, and the boner that had disappeared with the mention of Erin threatened to come back.

With a vengeance.

"She wanted to stay with Dallas—yes, that was his real name—and I wanted to get the fuck out of there, so we went our separate ways." I placed my hand over Bianca's. "And that's Erin for you."

I probably could've said more, told her about how I'd thought of traveling with Erin as the beginning of something amazing. Or about how disappointed I'd been when I'd realized I was wrong and that the beginning I'd wanted to stretch out into a long future was actually just the beginning of the end.

In some ways, we weren't so different, Bianca and me. We both thought we had something and as it turned out, we didn't. It's just that her relationship had a ton of history and mine had next to none, and because of that it wasn't fair to hold them side-by-side for comparison. Plus, I didn't want to give her a reason to not trust me or my judgment. Although, to be fair, she'd probably be right to do exactly that. It wasn't like I'd had a stellar record with women in the past. I was approaching my mid-thirties with a string of relationships behind me that, in hindsight, weren't even close to going the distance, and yet I'd thought pretty much all of them were *the one*. Erin was just the latest mistake I'd made.

I have to say, being a romantic sucked sometimes and not just because of the obvious fact that I'm a guy. Teasing and weird looks and disbelief aside, seeing connections that weren't there or that were tenuous as best sucked. Watching everything fall apart when my parents—all three of them—had given me these notions of what love looked like, this idea that it could just *bam*, hit you in a moment . . . it sucked. Really fucking sucked.

I turned my head away and closed my eyes, second-guessing myself for the first time. It was easy to say that Bianca was different, because it was true. She was. I could hold her up against all the other women I'd met and sensed a connection with over the years and comfortably say that she outpaced and outclassed them all. Beyond a shadow of a doubt.

But did that really mean what I thought it meant? Or was this just my softer tendencies setting me up to get hurt again? Only it wouldn't be again, because that implies the pain would be equal. And with the same certainty I could say that she outclassed the women of my past, I knew something else.

This woman could be the one to break me.

No. *No.* I focused on the feel of her hand underneath mine and tried to pinpoint what it was that made me so confident. It wasn't one thing though—it was several. Many. A whole hell of a lot. And not just physical things, like her smooth, soft skin that contrasted with my own, or her dark brown eyes that had been so sad and had started to come alive in front of me.

I considered hunting down a pen and a bit of paper to start a list, but Bianca reminded me that we'd been talking about my visiting Rose and how it hadn't happened. "But you didn't go see your sister after that?" she asked, curiosity lighting her eyes.

"Nah. I thought about it, but by then I knew that she was going to be home for Christmas. And since I'd sort of forgone a ton of things I'd wanted to do because of Erin, I decided to try to sneak some of that stuff in before I left. I talked to Rose, and she was cool with it." Leaning in, I whispered, "Actually, she suggested it. She'd met someone and I think she was secretly glad I wasn't coming there to play big brother on her."

"Would you have spied on her? Maybe threatened this someone?"

I huffed out a laugh. "Of course. It's my right as her brother. Plus," I added, because I didn't want Bianca to think I didn't care, "Rose's had it tough these last few years. I wouldn't want some dickhead wanker coming in and messing with her head."

"You mentioned that before. She's lucky to have you."

I nodded seriously. "She really is, it's true. What about you?"

"Am I lucky to have you?" She frowned comically. "Do I have you at all?"

"I meant do you think you're lucky to have your brothers," I clarified, remembering that she'd mentioned they lived in North Carolina. Biting my tongue, I couldn't help but wonder if the words I *wanted* to say were the right ones for the moment we were sharing. She was looking at me with wide eyes and a slight smile, her funny frown having transformed into an open expression that said she knew the weight of her question, inadvertent though it might've been.

Silence crept back in. My own doubts aside, I didn't want to say anything for fear of going too far with someone who was still recovering from broken trust and a broken heart.

And Bianca? I couldn't say why she didn't speak, though I'd like to think it was because she was hoping for the very thing I wanted to tell her.

That, in the end, I *did* tell her, because I couldn't hold back. "But yeah, pretty girl. I'd say you have me."

8

BIANCA

I HAD NO IDEA HOW TO RESPOND TO LUCAS.

Yeah, pretty girl. I'd say you have me.

It should've terrified me, but it didn't. God help me, it didn't—which I was sure I'd pick apart later, trying to figure out why. Acting on impulse, I leaned closer and brushed a kiss on his lips. It was light and soft and . . . I don't know. Maybe a promise? Because I couldn't return his words, but I could show him that he mattered.

Impossibly, after just a few hours, he mattered.

"What was that for? Not that I'm complaining, of course." His mouth tilted into a smile that was open, happy, and it made me feel adored.

Returning that smile, I shrugged. "No reason, you just looked like you needed it."

Cocking his head, he said, "Yeah? Tell me exactly the look I was giving you, so I can recreate it. You know, when I want another."

"No way. That'd be like giving you the keys to the kingdom."

Widening his eyes, he looked at me pleadingly, which

made me laugh. It felt like forever since I'd laughed as much as this. Crowded on the floor of an Airbus, winging our way to Australia—him returning to his family, me escaping mine —I was having more fun, was happier, than I'd been in years.

"So, now you know my sordid tale, what do we talk about next?" Lucas reached up and grabbed the end of one of my many, many curls, giving it a tug. The slight pull on my scalp zinged through my body and my brain short-circuited. Normally I'd be a little sensitive to someone just reaching up and pulling at my hair—for a long time I didn't love it like I should've, because of all the comments it garnered when I was a kid, not to mention what a pain it was to care for—but with him, I didn't mind.

The opposite, in fact. His eyes didn't hold derision but fascination and a little bit of longing. For him, my riotous black curls weren't a feature to be mocked, but another thing to appreciate about me.

Again, I wanted to say. *Harder.*

"Politics," is what I actually said.

The face Lucas gave me was priceless. If "fuck no" could be boiled down to one facial expression—that was it. "That looks like a hard no."

"What's harder than hard?"

Stifling a grin, I looked down at his lap pointedly, then brought my eyes back up to meet his gaze. "Um—"

"Maybe don't answer that," he interjected hurriedly. "That was not what I meant but kudos for making it about my dick."

I'm not too proud to admit that my eyes dropped again at the way he said "dick." It was thrilling, sending a shiver down my spine and a curl of straight-up *want* through my body. Without thought, I ran my tongue across my suddenly dry lips. "I-I-it-you're—are you getting hard?" After stumbling over what to say, the question escaped before I processed that I was going to ask it and I slapped a hand over my mouth to try and stop anything else from coming out.

I was pretty sure if I moved my hand an invitation to join the Mile High Club would follow, you see.

Would that be such a bad thing?

Lucas looked sheepish, bringing both of his hands to his lap in a lame attempt to cover himself. Because, yes, he was most definitely getting hard.

"In my own defense," he started, shifting slightly, "you're looking right at him and licking your sexy-as-fuck lips. He's a vain guy, he likes the attention."

Vain. Vein. Veins. Veiny.

I like it when they're veiny. I pictured my favorite GIFs and pictures—ones that I had saved in an album on my phone for when alone time rolled around—and wondered what Lucas' looked like.

Cut or uncut?

Did he have that big, juicy vein that I could trace with my tongue?

How would he taste, smell, feel?

"Where did your mind go? Because you've got this"—he lifted one hand to swivel around my face—"look that says it's nice there and maybe I should join you."

"I wasn't picturing your penis," I replied, because oh my god, the whole situation wasn't awkward enough.

On the bright side, we weren't talking about politics. A definite plus, because that shitshow had no place here. Not in this bubble of light-hearted, zingy attraction Lucas and I had formed.

He snort-laughed, turning his head away from me when

movement sounded from the other side of the curtains separating the galley from the rest of the plane. Someone shifting around and whispering—someone I was about 99.9% certain was headed for the facilities. And since we were still camped on the floor near the bathrooms, though I'd somehow turned my body so it shielded his from immediate sight, I knew we were only moments away from being caught.

Not that we were doing anything to get caught.

Were we? I had no idea if erections on airplanes were common, but I'd wager that, common or not, they were frowned upon.

I didn't want anyone frowning on my new friend.

And his smaller—but not small from the look of things—friend.

I leaned in to whisper, "Lucas, we should move," right at the same moment he turned back to me, our faces close enough to—

His lips were on mine in an instant, his mouth opening immediately when I swept my tongue out on instinct to taste him again. While my mind raced—the last kiss we'd shared had ended in me freaking out—my body responded by pressing closer, closer.

And my hand? It had a mind of its own. Like a freaking heat-seeking missile, it rocketed toward its target.

Do I need to tell you what its target was?

Lucas' cock. Hard, heavy and against the palm of my hand between one heartbeat and the next.

It's so hard! I'm not sure what I expected but the moment I wrapped my hand around him—as much as I could with his pants acting like a barrier—my thoughts degraded to simple, pathetic little exclamations. *It's so hot! I want it now!*

"Bianca." Lucas pulled back from our kiss—one that had

grown ever more heated as I slowly began to stroke him in an action that was the exact-fucking-opposite of what I'd intended to do.

I'd leaned in to tell him we were about to have our moment intruded on and should move and ended up with my tongue in his mouth and my hand on his grey-sweat-pants-covered cock.

But that didn't stop me. I started to move faster and faster over the length of him, wishing away those "trackie daks" that were far, far too sexy for their own good.

I was nearly mindless when I felt the first sting on my lower lip, barely any more cognizant when the second pinched me harder. *Biting me.* Lucas was biting me and instead of shaking me loose from my dick-induced haze, it just made me wonder if I could get away with sneaking my hand inside of his pants and gripping him for real.

Skin to skin.

His hot, hard shaft in my stroking palm.

Yes, yes, yes!

"Pretty girl, you have to stop," he groaned, his quiet words nearly lost in the gravelly, pained noise.

"I know," I replied, nodding even as I kept going, licking my lip where he'd bitten me and wondering what it would be like to be bitten in other places by him.

Jesus, take the wheel.

"Did you just ask for—oh, Jesus Christ, Bianca," he whisper-moaned as I added a little twist to my movement. His hand landed on mine, the pressure of it breaking both my concentration and my grip. Behind me, I could feel the presence of someone, and my face began to flush.

"You guys doing okay?" The feminine voice was soft and possibly a little amused.

Oh shit, how much had they seen?

Panic was a rising tide inside me, making all the words float away. In stunned silence, I watched as Lucas breathed deeply through his nose and gave a sleepy-looking smile at the woman behind me. "Yeah, fine. My girlfriend gets nervous on planes, so we thought we'd duck back here and stretch out a little."

"Oh, right. Don't let them catch you sitting back here." It didn't sound like she believed him, but other than her warning, she didn't say anything else and soon enough I heard the swish of a bathroom lock being slid into place.

I looked up at Lucas, his hand wrapped around mine still, and saw the dilated, almost dopey look in his eyes had returned after his brief, memorable performance for our not-so-adoring crowd. He had been—still was?—so turned on, his whole face had transformed, and I was so turned on I'd near jerked him to completion—*over his fucking pants*—in the back of the plane.

What the hell was wrong with me?

For one shining moment I actually felt a little surge of pride. I'd done something wild—even wilder than the kiss we'd shared—and though I knew it wasn't necessarily the best decision of my life, it had been mine. And my ex and his lingering mental voice were nowhere to be seen or heard. Only the pride wasn't to last. All too quickly I started to feel like I needed to escape again. But where to?

We'd made out in our seats.

Rounded third base in the galley.

Venturing to any other part of the plane seemed like a recipe for disaster. Lord help us if we ended up in, like, the cockpit.

"We should probably move," Lucas murmured, blinking rapidly as if trying to clear the haze. "She ducked into one of the free toilets but who knows who else is coming."

You, if we'd had two more minutes.

Nodding and already at the edge of my sanity, I whipped my head around, trying to think past my craziness. Except, it was impossible.

In fact, I must've completely lost my mind, because instead of being smart, instead of pulling back and thinking things through, I asked the question that had popped into my mind right around the time I'd first asked Lucas if he was hard.

"Think we can both fit in the bathroom?"

9

LUCAS

I BLINKED, MY MIND STILL SLUGGISH FROM BIANCA'S HAND AND her kiss and . . . *she was asking me if we'd both fit in the bathroom?*

After stroking me until I damn near came in my pants, she was asking me that?

As if the answer would be anything but a resounding, all-caps YES. The answer was yes even if it was technically a "no." Because there was no fucking way I was going to let the moment pass me by. Even if it meant I had to contort myself into a tight, tight place—pun once again intended.

"Lucas?" Worry carved a ripple between Bianca's eyebrows, her teeth sinking into her lower lip. "Are you angry?"

Startled at her question, I shook my head vehemently, the action clearing away the last of my haze. *Angry?* Hell no. I was painfully hard, turned on beyond belief, and in desperate, desperate need of touching her. But angry? Absolutely not.

"No, pretty girl." I lowered my voice, making absolutely certain that this private moment stayed that way. "But I was about twenty seconds away from coming and I'm not going to lie, stopping hurt. I need . . . I need . . ." I hesitated, suddenly aware of where we were, more so than I'd been since I'd told her she had me.

What was this woman doing to me that could make me forget myself?

"I know what you need," she whispered, her hand gripping mine. She tugged, a surreptitious look over her shoulder told me she was making sure the coast was clear.

It was, but for how much longer?

Pushing aside the fold-in door of the aeroplane bathroom she'd disappeared into after our kiss, she climbed atop the toilet lid, waving me in with her free hand while still holding on with the other.

I followed. Of course, I did. Despite some evidence to the contrary, I'm not an idiot.

"Bian—"

"Close the door, Lucas."

Nodding, I maneuvered my way around it, pushing it closed and sliding the lock into place. The light became brighter, but I didn't, couldn't, care about that. Not when, the second we were locked in privacy, Bianca dropped down to stand in front of me and brought her lips to mine. "Do you think anyone else saw us?" she asked against my mouth, the quiet words nearly lost to a kiss that I didn't know how to break.

That I didn't *want* to break.

"I don't know," I answered honestly, closing my eyes against the sensation of her lips on mine, again and again and again, in a series of soft, almost playful kisses. "Does it bother you?"

Please say no. If she'd said yes, I'd have stopped. It would have damn near killed me, but even if she was the one who'd started us down this path, I would be the one to end it if I thought it could cause her embarrassment or pain or regret.

I didn't want her to regret us.

I wanted her to want me like I wanted her.

And I wanted her to walk off this plane wanting me still. Again.

More.

Forever? Could I trust myself to answer that question after Erin and the others? I wanted to believe in what we'd started, damn it. I wanted to lean into it and into my stupid, hopeless romantic tendencies.

So, yes. Fucking forever.

"No. It doesn't bother me." She leaned back so our eyes could meet, and in hers I saw the truth. She was hot and getting hotter. And the risk factor was just feeding that heat. Fanning the flames. "It feels wrong but in the rightest way, Luc. How is that possible?"

Luc. Stupid that that's what I latched onto in her words, especially when she was basically admitting that the potential for people knowing what we were up to was part of the appeal—pretty, *dirty* girl. And yet, it hit me square in the chest, the way she said "Luc" with affection and trust and no small amount of need.

"Don't know, don't care." I smiled so she knew I was just as in the moment, and into the whole voyeur thing as she was, then let go of her hand so I could do what I'd been dying to do.

I thrust my hands into all that glorious hair, the curls gripping me as much as I gripped them. Making my hands into fists, I used my hold on her to tilt her head back and kiss her again.

Harder.

Wetter.

More demanding and more needy.

Her little whimper fueled me, the noise like a roar to my senses. She didn't have to say the word for me to know what that sound meant—*more*. She wanted more.

Thrusting my tongue into her mouth, reveling in her taste, I gave her hair the slightest pull—a test, to see if she wanted more.

She did. Her eyes, which had fallen closed when I brought our mouths together, flew open and were very nearly aflame. Like she was burning up on the inside and I was the accelerant.

Fighting hard against the impulse to just keep going, to always keep going, I tore myself away from the kiss . . . but refused to let loose the hold I had on those curls.

"Bianca, pretty girl, please. Please." I was begging but for what I didn't know.

I wanted to touch her, but I didn't want to let go my hold.

I wanted her to touch me, the idea of not kissing her anathema. At least until I pictured that mouth elsewhere.

Gliding down my chest, nibbling and biting and licking and sucking until she met the flexible waistband of my tracksuit pants and then . . .

"I want that. I want to put my mouth on you."

I might never know if she was responding to what she saw on my face—my fantasy written in my expression—or if I'd narrated my thoughts to her as they sprang into my head. Because in the next instant, she was gripping the hem of my T-shirt and tugging. Lifting it up and forcing me to let go of her, if only long enough for me to rip it off and shove it in the far corner of the bench, she started to do exactly what I'd envisioned.

Kissing my chest. Tonguing it. Using her teeth to scrape

over my nipple, making me shudder—fucking *shudder*—from the blaze that shot across my every nerve-ending.

"You're perfect, did you know that?" My words were soft, but my hands when I brought them back to those curls were anything but. I fisted them again, applying enough pressure to guide her lower, lower, lower, until she was seated on the toilet behind her.

A rough, harder scrape of her teeth, this time in the area below my belly button—an area I had no idea was so sensitive until her.

Until she bit me hard enough to leave a red mark.

Pressing her head back against my grip on her hair, she looked up at me, and I knew she was enjoying it, enjoying me, but that she didn't want to be rushed. Except I said, "I can't wait. I can't."

Maybe I should have tried harder to resist the lure of her lips. Maybe I should have manned-up and let her play. But . . . bloody hell. Her mouth was centimeters from my dick, and I was coiled so tightly, I thought I might just explode.

"Okay, Luc." Her words were gentle, while the accompanying smile was wicked. Still looking right at me, letting me see her pupils dilate, the brown of her irises—already so close to black—swept away in her desire, she brought her hands to the waist of my pants and pulled them down. Hard.

She dakked me. It was the stupidest, most inane thought of my life—the childish expression about an act that would've once caused complete and utter humiliation one I hadn't used since pantsing people was a funny/mean trick.

But then, her hands were on my arse, her nails clawing at me like she needed to hold me tight, and her mouth—

Oh fuck, fuck, fuck yes. Her mouth was surrounding me, the wet heat sinking down over my cock, spinning me into damn-near sensory overload.

My hands clenched, a muffled noise of protest reaching me as Bianca took me deep into the back of her throat, swallowing so the pressure was intensified until I thought I'd black out. And then . . .

And then she slowly started to draw her mouth back along my dick, sliding off at the tip with a pop and an "mmm, yes," that vibrated against the head. It felt, *fuck*, it felt so good that I was sure it was the end. That I was going to come on her face and mark her in the most primal of ways.

Why does that sound so good?

Why do I want that so bad?

"What are you thinking about?" Her voice was low and husky, her tongue darting out to swirl around the head of my cock as she looked up at me again. She looked like a goddess seated before me, my arms—hands still buried deep in her hair—bracketing my view of her, her lips swollen and wet, her hand visible as she brought it up to slowly stroke me while she waited for her answer.

Could I tell her what I wanted? What would she say if she knew what I was thinking?

Her skin, her warm brown skin that just begged to be licked and worshipped, painted with my cum.

I shook my head, afraid to share, because if she didn't want it too, then we might lose our moment and that moment was better than anything I'd ever experienced.

"Nuh-uh, Luc. You don't get to deny me now. I want to know what you're thinking." She held my eyes in thrall as she leaned in and wrapped her lips around my tip, her tongue caressing me, flicking me.

Without warning, she moved her head down, down, until she'd taken all of me again, bringing me to the back of her throat. She worked me over until I was panting and close again to coming, then drew off just as fast and bit her lip. Bringing her hands up, she used both to stroke me faster, her grip strong and firm, but not quite enough to get me there.

Not yet.

"What aren't you telling me, huh?" she mused, blinking at me in a way that told me she was unlocking a part of herself she'd kept hidden.

I didn't want to think why. Not then.

I just wanted—"I don't want to scare you," I confessed, the words ripped from my mouth when she pressed an innocent kiss to my hipbone, then skated her lips across to kiss the other. "I want . . ."

"You want to come, don't you? Where? Down my throat?" She slowed her hands and *looked* at me. I can't describe the way it felt to be looked at like that, by her. Like she could read everything about me and was judging exactly none of it. Her lips stretched into a filthy, knowing smile. "No, I don't think so."

Despite the fact that she already seemed to have me figured out, I still shook my head. Then nodded. Because *yes,* of course I wanted to come in her mouth. It just wasn't what I wanted right then.

"Do you want me to take my top off, Lucas? Let you come on my chest?" She looked down, my hands moving with her head as she contemplated the idea of me shooting on her tits. "Can you imagine how that might look, your cum on my skin? Because I can and I have to say"—she made a noise that was moan and hum combined—"I like what I'm picturing."

I blinked slowly, imagining her nipples with my seed dripping off them, closing my eyes completely to allow that scene to play on repeat behind my eyelids.

I felt the warm wet of her tongue swirling around my cockhead again, her demand for me to bring my attention back to her, perhaps? Not that she'd ever lost my attention—she'd just diverted it into a whole new fantasy that fifteen hours in a plane couldn't even begin to satisfy.

"Maybe another time for that. I think"—she paused, looking up at me with knowledge and mischief and naked desire, before licking her lips, oh so slowly—"I think you want to come on my face. Don't you?"

Don't you?

My heart stopped. My hands loosened their hold.

My eyes fell closed, my mind filling with graphic images of me doing exactly that.

I swore. Long and too loud when there could've formed a crowd of people just on the other side of the door.

I sucked in a long breath, opening my eyes to look down at her, so she could see exactly what she was doing to me.

And then, I nodded.

10

BIANCA

In my entire life, I'd never felt more powerful than I felt seated in front of Lucas, in control of both my body and his. It was heady, watching his reaction to me, tasting him on my tongue, asking him what he wanted—and giving it to him because I wanted to, and I could.

"Pretty girl," he gasped, green eyes filmed with a haze of need meeting mine in a desperate plea. He wanted to come, and he wanted to come on me.

On my face.

It was dirty—dirtier than anything I'd ever done with my ex, at least—and it felt forbidden. But I wanted it. Maybe even more than he did.

"Would you let me do that? Would you want that too?" The plea in his words was shot through with wonder, like he couldn't believe it.

And neither could I. In the far reaches of my mind, Mason tried to tell me this wasn't me—that I wouldn't, didn't, hadn't given him what he needed when he needed it, but I shoved him aside.

This moment was for me. And Lucas. This strange,

growing thing between us. Because, even as I nodded, confirming that yes, *yes*, I wanted it, and biting my lip so I didn't actually beg for it, I couldn't have imagined this moment with anyone else. *Anyone*. I might have been with Mason for years, but he wasn't Lucas.

Mason wasn't the one who made me lose myself and find myself at the same time. And he didn't belong on this flight with us.

Leaning in to suck on the tip of Lucas' dick, the salty hint of precum making me crazy—crazier—I wasn't yet ready to give up the power I held as surely as I held his thick, hard, veiny, perfect . . . but, *oh god*. I needed him to touch me. How could I make that happen? There was no room to move, crowded as we already were.

"Touch yourself." His voice cracked, his sexy accent stark, as he quietly gave me the direction that could have come from my own mind. *Yes*, I thought. Wanting to touch myself while I pleasured him, I slowly slid my hand off his dick to stand in front of him again. I needed only long enough to open my pants and push them down far enough to expose my underwear, but Lucas had other plans for me.

For us.

"I—I'm so wet, Luc. You did that to me."

He nodded, his hands still in my hair, his grip so wonderfully tight, I wondered if maybe he planned to hold on forever.

I didn't think I'd mind a forever with those sure hands holding me and touching me.

Using that hold on me to bring his lips to mine, he murmured, "I want to taste you."

But he didn't kiss me.

No. Instead, he held my gaze and used such words that I felt like I was spiraling into madness. "I want to spread you out in front of me, naked and pliable and so desperate for me, you'd do anything I asked. And then I'd part your legs and just look. *Look* at your pretty cunt. Because it is pretty, isn't it? A woman like you, so beautiful, so perfect—yeah, you'd have the prettiest pussy. You wouldn't be able to stop me from tasting you; you'd be begging for it. We wouldn't have these walls around us, so I'd be able to stretch out between your legs and once I'd finally, *finally*, looked my fill, I'd lick you. But slowly, because a pretty cunt should be savored, shouldn't it? I'd make sure I drove you wild and found out all the things you like best, and then"—he tugged on my hair, the pain so sharp it sent a spike of pleasure to my core—"and then I'd bite you. I want to bite you so bad, Bianca. Why? Why?"

I shook my head as much as his hands would allow, because I didn't know why. All I knew was that I wanted that too. I wanted it with a desperation that felt too big for the tiny bathroom that just barely concealed us from an airplane full of people.

"After I bit you, do you know what I'd do?" He pressed his lips to mine, the pause undoubtedly designed to make me crazy.

It worked. I heard myself whimper, wondering what scene he'd paint for me next, even as I brought one hand to the waistband of my panties and slid under, my finger seeking my clit and finding it swollen and sensitive. Realizing that the control I'd so relished was slipping from my grasp, I licked my tongue out to wet my lips and rolled my eyes back, moaning quietly because I wanted to draw his attention down—

And because I couldn't stop it from escaping.

Even with my eyes drawn to the ceiling, my head falling back because the combination of his words and my wetness, my finger and his hands in my hair, were making me weak, still I knew the moment he looked down.

And saw me rubbing myself beneath my panties. "Fuck, of course you're wearing white. Of course, you are, good little pretty girl."

I felt one hand in my hair loosen, his fingers gliding down my cheek, my neck, over my chest—which was rapidly rising and falling as my heart beat triple time—and down my stomach until they wrapped around my wrist. Firmly and unforgiving. "Do I get to touch you too?"

I started to shake my head, maybe just to be ornery, definitely because I wanted to see what he'd do, but he didn't let me. With the hand still wrapped up in my curls, he redirected me until I nodded. It was forceful and made my scalp tingle and I briefly thought that I should hate it—him taking that choice from me—but I didn't. I didn't.

Then his hand joined mine. I could still feel his phantom fingers circling my wrist, so strong his grip had been, and suddenly, all I could think about was him, tying me up. I wanted to ask him if he would—in his fantasy he'd just been narrating—but I didn't get a chance.

Not when his finger was pushing inside me, leaving me to keep working my pulsing clit.

Not when his lips were against my ear, whispering, "After I bit you, I'd fuck you with my tongue and my fingers until you screamed my name. Screamed it, pretty girl. Then I'd flip you over, pull you up onto your hands and knees and shove my dick so deep inside you, you'd feel me long after we'd finished."

"Yes, yes, yes, yes," I chanted, my hips rolling, my head turning in a mindless attempt to silence his dirty words with my kiss.

I just need to get my lips on his. Please, please.

"I'd fuck you hard, you know? Because how would I be able to stop myself? When you're on all fours in front of me, your back bare and waiting to be bitten. I'd bite you there too. All over, I'd bite. I'm obsessed with the idea of sinking my teeth into you." He paused, his finger stilling, then starting again, harder, harder. "I won't be happy until you let me."

"I'll let you." It was a near-soundless sob of words, my voice lost in the arousal that was holding my body hostage. "I want you to."

"I'd let you bite me too. If you wanted. Pretty girl, I'd let you do anything you want to me." He lowered his voice even further, until I couldn't even be sure I was hearing him, and said, "I'd even let you break me."

I couldn't fathom the trust it took to admit that. I wanted to ask him about it, beg him to explain what that meant and how I would do that and why, why would I do it, but I couldn't. I couldn't, because his finger kept pushing in and out of my body, only it wasn't one now. It was two, or maybe three, and I was so close. So close to coming that I was shaking, vibrating, my need making every part of my body feel raw and frantic and on edge.

"Luc, I'm there." I wet my lips again, startling when I felt his teeth on my tongue for an instant before he was kissing me uncontrollably, a frenzy of lips and teeth and tongues and—

"Oh, yes. *Yes. Yess.*" My pleasure-soaked moans were lost in his mouth, but I knew and he knew that I was riding the high of an orgasm so hard and so unexpected that my knees weakened as soon as the wave crested.

Sliding my hand free, I crumbled down until my ass hit the toilet behind me, looking up at him with wide eyes as our kiss broke. "Luc?" I needed to know what he was thinking, whether he was . . .

He reached down and circled my wrist again, this time drawing my hand up until he could close his lips around my finger and sucked, the tightness of his mouth sending another thrill of excitement through me. "Mmm, delicious," he whispered, his smile so wicked and mischievous that I desperately wanted to wipe it off his face.

And I knew just how to do it.

Pulling my hand free—not easily, but I didn't want it easy—I wanted him to mark me—I wrapped it around his still rock-hard cock and started stroking once more. "It's your turn again. Still?" Fluttering my eyes at him, I added, "You didn't get to come . . . on me. Yet."

He shuddered, his smile slipping just as I'd planned, to be replaced with a look so intense that I could've melted on the spot. Except I'd already melted for him. "Bianca—"

I cut him off with my mouth—bringing his dick to my lips to trace them, then opening and sucking him inside, inch by slow, torturous inch. Adding one hand to the base, I jacked him in time with my lips, my other hand reaching up to tug on his balls.

His hands.

Back in my hair.

My mouth.

Back on his dick.

I was ready to make at least one small part of his fantasy come true. And I wasn't stopping until he was done.

Moving my head up and down, my hand gripping him hard enough that he moaned, I swirled my tongue around his head, delighting in the taste of his precum as it began to leak from his tip faster, and faster. Until his fists pulled me back, his eyes afire as he looked down at me and said, “Now.”

Bringing both hands to his cock, I jacked him, aimed him, watched him, and waited.

And when I felt the first warm, sticky pulse of him on my skin, I smiled, reveling in the way I’d made him lose control. And in the way he’d made me feel.

The moment seemed to hang; the air hot from the way we combusted.

“You’re beautiful.” Lucas’ voice was edgy yet gentle, his hands coming to cup my cheeks. With the smallest amount of pressure, he raised my face to his, the look in his eyes intense. “God, look at you.”

I bit my lower lip. An involuntary reaction because I was suddenly feeling exposed and vulnerable and—

“Hey, are you okay? Did I . . . ?” His question trailed off as he shifted slightly, reaching for the paper towel dispenser with one hand, keeping the other warm against my flushed cheek.

My flushed, cum-coated cheek. No need to skirt around that fact. After all, I’d all but begged Lucas for it, and he’d obliged me in the most viciously, perfectly sexy way.

God, I could come again just thinking about it. But first, I needed to reassure him. “You didn’t upset me, or do anything I didn’t want, if that’s what you’re thinking.” I smiled, the sticky feel of him on my skin making my body clench and tighten, even though I’d just been thoroughly satisfied by the man in front of me.

The man who was now using warm water to wet the paper towel so he could, I assume, wipe the evidence of his pleasure from my skin.

“You got quiet,” was all he said, his eyes switching from

intense to focused as he carefully ran the rough paper over my cheeks, across my lips and up to my forehead.

Let's just say his orgasm was *explosive*, shall we? I'd shut my eyes against the force of it, not because I didn't want to see it, but because I didn't want to catch any cum in my eye.

I had it on very good authority that that shit burned. I didn't need to find out firsthand to believe it.

When he threw the paper towel into the sink behind him, I reached out to grip his forearm—taking a moment to marvel at the corded muscle there—needing his attention completely on me.

"Bianca?" His voice was soft as he turned back toward me, and I was startled to realize that he was feeling exposed and vulnerable too.

"I've never done anything like that. And I know that's cliché, but I need you to know it's true. With you, I just . . . it felt right. And good. And I wanted everything we did. More. I wanted *more*."

"Yeah?"

"Oh, yeah." I stood, feeling a rush of affection for Luc when he cupped my cheeks again, his thumbs smoothing back and forth across my cheekbones. "You got to tell me your fantasy. Shall I tell you mine?"

He nodded, a small smile forming on his delicious mouth, and it was impossible to resist a quick kiss. Which soon became a deeper, hotter, wetter kiss when he used his hold on me to tilt my head for better access. Breathing heavily, I pulled back, only because I knew that if I didn't, we'd be having sex in the airplane bathroom within minutes and . . . I wasn't sure if I was ready for that yet.

I wasn't sure I *wasn't* ready either, though.

"Tell me," he whispered against my lips before nipping at my bottom one. It was quick, a shallow bite that reminded me of his dirty words, his admitted obsession with biting me.

"Turn first." I shifted slightly, using my body to indicate that I wanted him to trade places with me. What followed was a funny little dance as we tried to navigate the small space while both us were a mess of partially removed clothes and exposed body parts. I stopped his attempt to tuck his cock back into his sweatpants because I wanted to be the one to do it.

I had to be the one. It seemed necessary, so I went with it.

Surprisingly, Lucas didn't complain. Possibly because I made sure to be tender as I wrapped a hand around him, reveling in the way he responded to my touch with a moan that was throaty and needy and not at all the moan of a man who'd just come all over my face.

"Why, Lucas Hawke," I said, no small amount of wonder in my voice, "do you want me again?" I punctuated the question with a light stroke of his dick before using my free hand to pull forward on the waistband of his pants, ready to tuck him away.

He was shaking his head before I'd even released him, and my heart thudded to a stop. Did he not want me now he'd had me like this, tucked away in the bathroom of an airplane, far from the day-to-day realities of life?

"When did you stop wanting me and start wanting her?"

I started to take a step back, shuddering against the echo of my too-small question, the one I hadn't wanted to ask of Mason but had *needed* to know the answer to. I couldn't help but wonder if I'd read something wrong in our situation, mine and Lucas', but before I could get too lost inside my own head, Lucas was pulling me closer. "No. Not again, pretty girl."

"No?"

"Not again. Always."

Heat flamed up my spine, sending the signal to every part of my body that we were *ready*. His words, the simple way he seemed to accept this thing between us . . . it might be the sexiest thing about him, and the man had a goddamn Australian accent.

He could ask me to take the trash outside in that accent and my panties would fall off. At least, I was pretty sure that's what would happen.

Still reeling a little—from the orgasm he'd given me, the orgasm he'd painted on my face, the words he'd offered me that said that this connection between us was no small thing —I hauled his lips to mine for another kiss.

This time, it was him who broke it. "You said you were going to tell me your fantasy."

I fluttered my eyes at him, trying to affect a look of innocence that I knew he wasn't buying the moment he slid one hand down from my cheek to my chest, pinching one of my nipples with a stern, "Tell me, pretty girl."

Like I could resist that.

"Hmm, well, it starts with you naked and me naked and ends happily," I teased, my head falling back as he began to play with my peaked nipple, plucking it through my shirt, circling it with a fingertip, pinching it tightly between thumb and forefinger. "Shit, Luc."

"I'll stop if you stop." It was a warning, a threat. He wasn't going to stand for my teasing, and I wasn't going to let him kill my pleasure. Not yet.

Not ever.

"I'd push you onto a bed," I started, only to be interrupted.

"Whose bed?"

I tilted my head, the movement dislodging the hand that still cupped my cheek, which Lucas then brought to my neglected breast to start giving my other nipple the same treatment as the first. "Mine. My bed."

"Yeah. Is your bed big enough for me?"

I nodded.

"Then what? After you've pushed me onto the bed?"

"I'd watch while you ran your hand up and down your cock. I'd make you jerk off for me, until you were close, and then I'd make you stop."

"And just how do you plan"—he paused, pinching both my nipples at the same time—"to make me stop?"

I sighed out a moan, blinking my eyes which were refusing to focus. I just wanted to roll them up, drop my head back and let the feel of Lucas take me away. Again.

"No answer? Come on, don't be shy." Removing his fingers from my breasts, he dropped his already-quiet voice. "Remember, you stop, I stop."

"I'd climb onto the bed and stop you with my body. I'd straddle you so you'd find it hard to keep moving your hand on your cock. Maybe I'd rub myself on you, on the back of your hand, so you'd be able to feel how wet watching you made me."

"I like that idea. Keep going." He ran a hand up my side and across the top of my chest, near my collarbone. "Would you raise up enough so I could turn my hand over and put my fingers in you? I know you like it when I have my fingers in you." Another raised eyebrow, his cocky expression reminding me of the very forward way he'd asked me if I'd liked what I'd seen when he'd caught me checking him out. All the way at the start of our flight. Mere hours ago, I reminded myself, though it felt like it could've been forever. That's how comfortable I felt with him.

Head spinning again, the change in my thoughts as sudden as they'd been when we'd first kissed, I closed my eyes and tried to conjure up an answer to the question that had chosen that moment to plague me.

I couldn't find it, the answer I was looking for. "Lucas?" I asked instead, hoping perhaps he had what I needed.

He had to have noticed the change in my body language, in my voice, because his hand stilled immediately. "Bianca?"

"Is this real?"

"You and me?"

I nodded, a wave of worry trying to crash through our moment. "It feels real, but how can it be?" I left unsaid all the doubts that plagued me—about how we hadn't known each other anywhere near long enough, about how I'd been wrong, so wrong, with Mason. About how it turns out that even thirteen years of marriage isn't enough to know someone, so how could not much more than thirteen hours be any better?

Instead of giving me an immediate answer, he fell back on the toilet lid, reached out to grab me and pull me onto his lap. "I can't answer that."

I liked his honesty—preferred it to some bullshit answer that told me only what he thought I wanted to hear—but still. Everything about what was happening to us was challenging my ideas about myself and about lust and love and fate and forgiveness.

I wondered about Mason. Had he ever felt like this about me? I knew from almost the moment Lucas sat down next to me that there was something different about him, but I couldn't, wouldn't, have predicted this.

Me, perched on his lap, freshly satisfied and ready to be satisfied some more. Willing to share my dirty thoughts and fantasies with him, because I trusted him to take care with them. To make them come true, even.

Lucas wrapped his arms all the way around my waist, pulling me in and holding me close. "I think it's as real as we make it."

Nodding, because yes, that made sense, I moved on to the next question that I wanted—*needed*—an answer to.

"What happens when the plane lands?"

What happens when the plane lands?
Find out in *The Arrival of You*

Available October 16, 2019

How long does it take to fall in love?

Bianca Evers learned the hard way—after thirteen years with her ex-husband—that not even half a lifetime of love is enough to save her from heartbreak. So the idea of falling for someone in less than fifteen hours? *Impossible.*

Lucas Hawke is under no illusion that the beautiful American he fell for on their flight to Australia feels the same. She might want him—but just like the women in his past, she's only thinking of right now.

But sometimes fate intervenes.
And sometimes someone arrives in your life who is meant to stay.
Forever.

ACKNOWLEDGMENTS

It takes a village to write a book, and my village is populated with the most wonderful people. Family and friends and colleagues alike. I'd be here forever if I tried to thank them all, so let me just say this instead—

Thank you for listening to me, supporting me, encouraging me and believing in me. I appreciate it more than you'll ever know.

ABOUT THE AUTHOR

B. Cranford is a proud Australian living in the USA, a lover of books, breadsticks and bed, and the mother of two children who are far too similar to their father for her liking. A lifelong reader, she dove into the romance genre on the recommendation of her best friend and hasn't looked back since. After three years as a blogger, she decided it was high time she finally finished one of the 12,002 books she'd started writing, and the end result was her debut novel, *The Brightest Star*.

Visit Beth at http://bcranford.com to stay up to date or follow her online:

- bookbub.com/authors/b-cranford
- facebook.com/bcranfordauthor
- twitter.com/bcranfordauthor
- instagram.com/bcranfordauthor
- goodreads.com/bcranford
- amazon.com/author/bcranford

ALSO BY B. CRANFORD

RESCUED BY LOVE

She Found Him

She wasn't looking but still . . . she found him.

She Hated Him - Available 2020

She hated him . . . and the way he made her feel.

THE AVENUE

About Time

It's all about timing . . .

Because Forever

Everyone should have a chance at forever . . .

For Today

First comes love, then comes marriage . . .

BRIGHT & CRAZY

The Brightest Star

The biggest gamble he ever took was leaving . . .

A LITTLE BIT CRAZY

She thinks they're enemies, he knows they're something more . . .

A CRAZY CHRISTMAS

If they can make it through the holidays, they can make it through anything . . .

Made in the USA
Columbia, SC
04 March 2020

88734102R00069